SUPREME & JUSTICE 2

ERNEST MORRIS

Good2Go Publishing

Supreme & Justice 2
Written by Ernest Morris
Cover Design: Davida Baldwin
Typesetter: Mychea
ISBN: 9781943686490

Published 2017 by Good2Go Publishing
7311 W. Glass Lane • Laveen, AZ 85339
www.good2gopublishing.com
https://twitter.com/good2gobooks
G2G@good2gopublishing.com
www.facebook.com/good2gopublishing
www.instagram.com/good2gopublishing

 This story is a work of fiction. Characters, businesses, places, and events and incidents are either the product of the author's imagination or used in a fictitious manner. Any resemblance to actual persons, living or dead, is purely coincidental.

ACKNOWLEDGEMENTS

First and foremost, I have to thank God once again for keeping me focused long enough to produce another novel.

Second, I would like to thank all my readers for supporting me, and keeping me motivated to bring you into my world whether it be fiction or non fiction.

There's so many friends and family members to thank that I may forget , or would be writing forever, but if you have supported me in any way, I thank you.

Special thanks goes out to Googd2Go Publishing for continuing to believe in me.

Thanks to my kids for staying focus in school, as well as life all together. Thanks to their mothers for being so strong and devoted.

Shout out to: Hassan Akbar, Footie, LS, Lex, Knowledge, Doe, Skin, Jay, Omar, Peanut, Mike Mike, Sheed, Feece, Lonnie, Triz, Nut, Rafiq, Du, Whoopie, Mayo, Ice Merv, Devon, Ray, Turtle, Mr. Johnson,

Frank, Jahad, Dominique, Worlds, Bub, Leneek, Dwunna, Rasheed, Theresa, Maurice, The Yunk, Alona, Kimyetta, Gianni etc. Anyone else that I forgot to mention, it wasn't intentional, but thank you also.

DEDICATION

I dedicate this book to all the men and women just coming home, or that's on their way home from doing time in prison. It's a new day and we need to cherish this opportunity because there may not be another.

You may feel that someone owes you something, and your pride may get in the way, but think about where you came from and all the obstacles that you had to overcome. Use that as your motivation to take the necessary steps forward, instead of going backwards. Remember for every action, there's a reaction, and for every reaction, there will always be consequences. What I'm saying is, don't come home with the same mentality that you went in with. It can only lead to two things, you going back to prison, or six feet under. Either way you will lose and they will win.

BE SAFE AND ENJOY FREEDOM!!!!!

PROLOGUE

Supreme and Justice

Gina had no choice but to break down and tell Supreme about her so-called relationship with his brother. She even told him about how she was accused of being a whore. Supreme actually believed that part because she was just about to probably fuck him and his mans.

"I'll give you his address, but I'm not going over there," she said.

"You're going to take me to my brother," Supreme said, pulling his gun out.

He was really scaring the shit out of her now. She didn't know what he would do next, so she agreed, hoping he would put the gun in his hand away.

"I will go with you and stay in the car. Can I at least tell Walid I'm going with you?"

Before Supreme could respond, the front door flew open, and two men wearing ski masks busted in, guns in hand. “Get the fuck on the floor,” one of them shouted.

Thinking quickly, Supreme grabbed Gina to use as a shield, then pulled her close to him, behind the wall. He already had his own gun out, so he pointed it at her head. “You niggas picked the wrong fucking house to rob.”

Justice couldn’t believe his eyes. He knew he just didn’t see his twin brother and his old chick duck behind that wall. He looked at Tank with a confused expression on his face. “What the fuck is going on?” he asked.

Tank shrugged his shoulders and started walking toward the area where Supreme and Gina were, aiming his gun.

Justice grabbed his arm. “Chill the fuck out; dude is my brother.”

Supreme was standing there debating if he should just go out in a blaze of glory, but the peeps were not moving. It all made sense to him now. “Bitch you set us up, didn’t you?”

Gina didn’t reply. She just stood there in a hysterical trance, wondering what was about to happen to her. She wasn’t ready to die. “Somebody please help me,” she screamed.

“Shut up!” Supreme smacked her over the face with the butt of his gun, then slowly moved from behind the wall, with Gina in front of him, the gun pointed at her head. “Drop your guns or I’m a give this bitch a wig shot.”

When Tank saw the gun aimed at Gina’s head, he regretted ever setting up the whole thing. He wished he would have listened to Donte. What fucked him up even more was, the nigga holding the gun looked exactly like Justice.

“It’s me, bro,” Justice said, lowering his gun, and pulling his ski mask off. When Supreme saw his brother’s face, a million emotions shot through him. He was happy, mad, and confused. He didn't know what to do or how to feel at the moment. It took every fiber in his body not to drop his gun and embrace his brother, but right now he had to stand his ground. He had no idea what was going on.

"Aye, big bro!" Supreme said with a sinister laugh. "Shit changed. We ain't babies no more. I only love the streets, so drop the guns or I'm gonna kill this scheming bitch." He thought Justice still had love for Gina, so he tried using her to his advantage to defuse the situation.

Justice looked Gina dead in the eyes. "I don't give a fuck about that bitch, kill her ass."

When Tank heard Justice say that, he knew he had to do something, and fast. He stepped out in front of Justice, then tossed his gun on the floor. "Aye, Justice, this your brother, dawg. It was just a big misunderstanding. Let's be out."

"You trippin', nigga. Shit can't go back to normal now," Justice replied, never taking his eyes off his brother.

Tank looked over to Supreme and tried to reason with him. “Just let her go, man. We didn’t know it was you.”

That seemed like the reasonable thing to do, Preme thought, but somebody needed to pay for trying to rob him. “If I let her go, it will be her hitting the ground from catching a hot one to the dome.”

“Come on, man! You don’t have to do this,” Tank pleaded.

Out of the corner of his eye, Supreme noticed Walid creeping down the steps with an assault rifle cocked and ready to go. Knowing he had the upper hand now, he pushed Gina on the ground, then looked at his brother, Justice. “Sorry we had to meet like this, bro.”

Boom! Boom! Boom!

And now the sequel: Supreme & Justice II

SUPREME
&
JUSTICE 2

CHAPTER 1

"What the fuck just happened?" Justice said, ducking down from the gunshots. When he looked up Supreme was holding the smoking gun. He turned to see a body sprawled out on the steps. He had no idea the other person had the drop on him.

"I just saved your ass," Supreme replied, looking at his best friend and mentor lying dead in a pool of blood.

Justice didn't respond. He dropped his gun and rushed over to his brother. The two embraced briefly, and then Justice snapped out of the sentimental stage he was in and got back to business.

"This muthafucka tried to set us up?" Justice said, staring in Gina's direction.

Gina wasn't paying any attention because she was too busy throwing up in the corner. She had never seen a man die before, especially in front of her. Everything that could go wrong, just went wrong. She wiped her face, then looked at Justice with pleading eyes. "I, I'm sorry fo—"

Before she could get the rest of her words out, Justice punched her dead in the mouth. Gina hit the floor so hard, she hit the back of her head on the wall. She grabbed her head in pain.

"Bitch, you got some fucking nerve saying anything to me. You're a snake," Justice said, then looked at Tank, who was standing there biting his bottom lip. "Did you know who she wanted us to rob?"

"Fuck no! They just said it was a couple of niggas getting money," he admitted. Tank was enraged at the sight of his girl lying on the ground spitting her teeth out. It wasn't supposed to go down like that, and now he was regretting it. He wished she would have left like he told her to.

"Man, kill that bitch," Supreme shouted, cocking his gun.

Justice looked at Gina momentarily, then turned

toward Supreme. His brother looked the same as when they were kids. The only thing was different now was, Supreme still had his long braids, and Justice had waves.

"We have to get out of here," Tank said, trying to save Gina's life.

Supreme wasn't trying to hear any of the shit he was talking. He didn't like the fact that a bitch caught him slipping like that. He walked right up to Gina and put three bullets in her chest. "Now let's get out of here! Bro, help me grab the money and work," he said to Justice.

They grabbed everything, then rushed out of the house. Tank was pissed and wanted to kill Preme for killing his girl, but that only meant he would have to kill his brother too. He decided to wait until the time was right; then he would get his revenge.

~ ~ ~

Supreme and Justice were sitting in Kreasha's crib catching up on everything that happened over the last twelve years. They were so deep into their conversation, they never saw Kreasha's friend come in until she walked past and spoke.

"Damn who was that?" Supreme asked, staring at her ass. She had on a pair of tight fitting capris that left almost nothing to the imagination.

"Oh that's Lena. That bitch is easy, bro! You can definitely hit that if you want it," Justice said with a smile.

"I just might have to."

"So what are you getting into today?"

"Well, I still have a business to run. I have to meet my connect in about an hour. How about you take that ride with me? That way I can introduce you to him. There is one thing, bro. I need you to leave that robbing shit alone, and rock with me. We can really control these cities, bro," Supreme replied seriously. "You don't have to do that shit anymore. Together, we will have shit on smash, and nobody will be able to fuck with us."

"I hear you, but I want to bring in some niggas I trust also. They've been rocking with me since the beginning."

"As long as they're not on that type time anymore. Come on so we're not late meeting up with bull," Supreme replied, heading for the front door.

~ ~ ~

When they pulled up in front of the house, Justice looked around at how perfect it looked. The grass was greener than he had ever seen. There were guards walking around with earpieces in their ears and assault rifles hanging from their shoulders. "These niggas on some Scarface shit, bro. This muthafucka is guarded like the White House," he said, looking at the men staring at them as they exited the car.

Supreme had a smirk on his face because that's the same way he felt when he first came here with Walid. He rang the doorbell and was greeted by a beautiful Hispanic woman wearing a tight-fitting maid uniform.

"Come in, gentlemen," the maid said, walking away.

They walked behind her, trying not to stare at her ass. They were escorted into the dining hall where Carlos was sitting reading the newspaper. He motioned for them to have a seat, then sat the paper on the table. The Spanish woman that answered the door, left the room.

Seconds later another woman even prettier than the first entered. "¿Qué quieres comer?" she asked as she placed three menus on the table.

"I'll have the picadillo con huevos. Grácias," Carlos said before closing up his menu.

"¿En qué puedo servirle?" She turned her attention to Justice and Supreme, who both were looking dumbfounded.

"What do you want to eat?" Carlos chimed in, helping them out. "They only speak Spanish, my friend!"

"Oh, okay," Justice said, finally understanding.

"Let's see, I'll have some eggs, tea, and a couple slices of toast."

Carlos translated what Justice had said into Spanish for the maid. Supreme ordered the same thing as his brother.

The lady smiled, staring at the two handsome young men. "Grácias, señor." She took the menus on her way back to the kitchen.

"Damn, you really have it going on in here," Justice stated. "I wish I had beautiful women waiting on me hand and foot."

"I'm just fortunate to have such a loyal staff, that's all. Loyalty is everything," Carlos said.

"I couldn't agree with you more," replied Supreme.

After the beautiful female brought out a tray with chips and salsa then left again, Carlos got down to business. "You were saying something about Walid no longer being in the game?"

Supreme broke down everything that happened,

leaving out the part about Justice trying to rob them. He didn't want Carlos to second-guess the arrangement they previously had. Carlos listened intently as Supreme made Walid look like a snake. Carlos believed every word.

"I always knew something was up with that kid. That's one of the reasons I never dropped anything heavy on him," Carlos started, dipping a chip in the salsa. "That day I met you, I could tell by your eyes you were hungry for the game. Walid only spoon-fed you, but I'm going to let you eat as much as you can handle. I sense no deceit in you, Preme."

"I never bite the hand that feeds me," Supreme replied.

"I'm not feeding you anything. I'm just a man that can supply you with whatever you need. It's up to you how you eat. You can make a lot of money fucking with me, my friend. I am very well connected from California to New York." Carlos sparked up a Cuban cigar. He held the smoke in for a minute, then slowly let it out. "Have you ever seen a ton of heroin?"

"No, sir, I don't believe I have," Supreme said. "However I've always believed one day I would, before all this shit happened."

"Let me explain something to you, Preme. You could be sitting on millions right now and couldn't buy a ton of heroin if you didn't have the right connections." Carlos shook his head. "Money ain't worth nothing if you can't make it grow."

Justice sat there listening to the conversation, staring at his brother. It was like he had never known him. He had grown into a superb businessman, and watching him made Justice realize just how well they were going to mesh. Supreme would handle the business aspect, and he and his crew would be the muscle.

"So what do you have in mind?" Supreme asked.

Carlos put out his cigar, then stood up from the table. He walked over to a picture hanging on the wall.

He slid it to the side, displaying a keypad. When he typed in a bunch of numbers, the wall opened up. Supreme and Justice stood there fascinated at what they saw. They had never seen so much dope in their lives. It was wrapped in wax paper, and was stacked neatly from the floor to the ceiling.

"This is what I have in mind for you and your brother," Carlos said with his arms stretched out. "Are you ready to really lock shit down?"

They looked at each other, then at all the dope. As if their minds were in sync with one another, they both turned toward Carlos. "Hell yeah!" they blurted out simultaneously.

CHAPTER 2

Tank was in his room looking at pictures on his cellphone he had taken of Gina. It has been over two months since her death, but the pain was still there. He thought back to the first time they had sex:

Summer of 2016

"What's up with you?" Tank asked, watching Gina eat a freeze pop.

"Shit!" she replied. "Where is your brother at?"

"Him and Chris went to play basketball. They'll be back in an hour or so."

"Okay, well tell him I came bye and he needs to answer his phone when I call," she said, heading for the door.

"Hold up for a minute," Tank said, walking toward her. "Word on the street is, you about getting at the dollar."

"What you talking about?"

"You know what I'm talking about," he said, pulling out some money.

Gina looked at the money, then looked at Tank. She thought about what he was asking for a moment, then stared at the money. She figured since she was here and he was offering, she would oblige. "You better not tell your brother, and I'm serious," Gina said, throwing the freeze pop in the trash can. "Who's here?"

"Nobody!"

"Make sure the door is locked," she told him, sitting down on the couch.

Tank was excited about what they were about to do. He hurriedly checked the door, then rushed over to the couch where Gina was.

"Where's my money?" she asked, holding her hand out.

Tank peeled off three twenties, then passed them to

her. She tucked them away in her purse.

Tank scooted down in front of her, spreading her legs apart. He began rubbing her pussy through her panties. "You like that?" he whispered, paying special attention to her clitoris.

"Mmmmmm," Gina replied. She closed her eyes, grabbed his hand, and started working it over her mound. Tank pulled off her panties, then pulled his shorts down to his ankles. He entered her with slow strokes, then sped up the pace.

"Oh shit," she moaned, opening her legs wider for him.

The warmness coming from her pussy made Tank tense up. He knew he was about to cum, so he turned her over, entering her from behind. A couple of minutes later, he was shooting his load deep inside her. Gina went into the bathroom to wipe herself, while Tank pulled up his shorts. When she came out, they made a deal to continue doing it as long as the money was right.

Gina told him he better not ever let Justice find out, then left out the house.

"Tank," Chris yelled, snapping him out of his daydream.

"What's up?"

"Come on, Justice is waiting for us."

Tank hopped off his bed and threw on his shoes. Chris stood in the door, anxiously waiting for him. They were about to meet Supreme and Justice to talk about the business. Justice had convinced his brother to let them be a part of the team, along with Dominique and Donte.

"Dom and Donte are already at the trap house waiting too," Chris told him as they jumped in the Grand Marquis Tank bought a week ago.

It only took them twenty minutes to get to the house. Everyone was there and ready to get down to business. Supreme kept staring in Tank's direction because he really didn't trust him, especially after what had gone down. He knew he would have to keep an eye on him. If it came down to it, he wouldn't hesitate to put him down.

"First and foremost, before I announce what our plan is, is there anyone that don't want to be a part of this?" Supreme looked around, but no one spoke up. "Once you're in, there's no turning back. I'm not trying to hear any bullshit, because I won't tolerate it. Me and my brother will run this operation with a iron fist. Right now we have Delaware and Philly on smash. I'm trying to take over all of the different cities in PA as well."

"How do you suppose we do that?" Donte responded. "That means there will be a lot of blood shed."

"Exactly my point. That's where y'all come in at."

"That's what I'm talking about. I'm always on go mode," Tank replied, rubbing his hands together.

"Only if it's necessary, okay? First we try compromising with them. If that doesn't work, Justice, you and your team can do what you do best."

Justice gave his twin a nod letting him know he understood. When it came to putting in work, they were always precise and took drastic measures so they never got caught.

"So what's up with getting this money?" Dominique asked, wanting to hear some good news.

"I was just about to get to that," Supreme countered. "I want to have weight flowing out of one crib, and bundles in another. The third crib will have the single baggies. All the traffic will come thru us and no one else. If niggas want to do their own thing, they can, as long as the work still comes from us."

Supreme knew what it took to run such an operation. It took leadership and dedication! A leader couldn't show any signs of weakness because the people following would try to take advantage if that happened. He was taught by one of the best, and nothing was going to stop his money flow.

"So who will be where?" Justice inquired.

"I will let you decide where you put your people at. My main concern is getting the work and making sure these streets are flooded with the best dope in the city. I know y'all were tired of sticking niggas up not knowing what you would be getting away with. I can promise you this though, if you stick with us," he said, pointing at himself and Justice, "we will all be rich in no time."

Supreme and Justice looked around the room and saw the seriousness in all their faces, except for Tank. Supreme could look into his eyes and see deceit written all over his face. The only thing was, he still couldn't figure out why.

"How about we keep the bundles and the baggies pumping out of the same spot, and we can push some loud out of the third one?" Donte said.

"That's a good idea," Justice added.

"Well, that's it, then. We are all going to come up, I assure you. I have to go meet up with my connect so I can get him to expand my order. Justice will get y'all set up with the trap houses you will be in charge of. Watch yourselves when y'all out in Philly. We're going to stir up a lot of trouble out there once our shit is the only thing pumping," Supreme stated.

"I thought you already had shit on lock out there?" Tank said sarcastically.

"I do," Preme shot back. "Once I put out this pure shit and lay a couple of those fiends down, it's going to stop all the other dealers' flow. If you can't handle this type of shit, there's the door."

"Come on, y'all," Justice intervened because he didn't want to have to choose sides between his twin and adoptive brother—it wouldn't be a choice.

"I'll hit y'all when I get back. This will be one of our main meeting spots. We will wrap and bag everything up here for Delaware, and the crib out West Philly for PA, then distribute it to all the spots in those areas." Supreme stated, heading out.

"Bro, let me holla at you real quick," Justice said,

stepping out with him.

"What's up?"

"You a cold piece of work. You see how they was eating that shit up?"

"Everybody looks like they're hungry, but you need to keep an eye on that nigga Tank. There's something about him I don't like."

"He's cool, bro; I'm telling you. He's with us," Justice replied.

"My gut says otherwise, but I hope you're right. I have to go, but get them out there collecting that gwap from the workers. Anything comes up short, that's on them," Preme told him, hopping in his car.

Justice headed back inside to give everyone the area they'll running. He could also now since the malice in Tank's heart. He knew from being around his brother in this short time, if he had some suspicion about someone, it warranted some looking into. He would keep an eye on him to make sure.

CHAPTER 3

One of Justice's blocks in Delaware was chirping, but the majority of the money was going to the opposite side of the street. They were getting a lot of the clientele that came through the block. He was able to get that side because Malik used to sell dope there. A couple of days ago, Malik was arrested on gun charges and was looking at twenty years as a third-time offender. Now it was just his young bulls out there, so Justice decided to let them work for him. He gave the lieutenant job to his adoptive brother Chris, and was waiting for him to arrive.

Ring! Ring! Ring! His cellphone went off. It was Kreasha.

"What's up with you, sexy?"

"I have a surprise for you. Come to my house real quick. It's an emergency!"

"I'm on the block right now, Kreasha," Justice

replied.

"I won't keep you long. Check the message I sent you."

Justice looked at the message that just came through, and got excited. He told her he would be there soon, then ended the call. He called one of his workers over to watch shit while he made a quick run.

"You're in charge until Chris gets here. He's stuck in traffic but will be here soon," he told the kid before hopping in his car. The young bull rushed back over to finish serving the fiends.

~~~

Kreasha eyes rolled into the back of her head. Sweat ran from her forehead, all the way down to her nipples. With her hands planted on his sweaty chest, she rode his hard dick like it was the last one she'd ever ride. His veins popped out of his forehead while he gasped for air. The swooshing sound her pussy made only added to the sensation.
~~~

"Yesss! Yesss," she moaned while she worked his cum right out of him.

"I'm about to cum!" she heard him holler, and hopped off his dick, trying to catch his hot load into her mouth.

"Ummm," she moaned as she jacked his dick into her mouth. His warm sperm was soothing going down her throat.

Pulling his dick out of her mouth, she turned onto her side, and opened her legs so he could hit it sideways. Her inner thighs and pubic hairs were smeared with thick white cum from her own orgasm. With her left leg over his shoulder, she gripped his ass and guided him inside her warm pussy. It made his half-limp dick stand at attention again. Kreasha held onto his waist as Justice stroked her hard, making sure he hit the right spot. She grunted, moaned, groaned, and begged for him to go deeper.

She reached up and grabbed her ankles, spreading

her legs wider so her pussy could stretch out for his huge shaft. Sweat dripped off his face into her mouth, but she was too far in the zone to notice. She kept her eyes closed tight, with her mouth wide open, waiting to erupt. When Justice pulled out of her, cum was still dripping off the head of his dick.

"Come here," she said, reaching for his dick. She put it into her mouth, sucking all the juices off of it. When she removed it from her mouth, it was clean, except for a little saliva on the head.

"So that was the surprise you had for me, huh?" Justice said, grabbing his clothes off the floor next to the bed.

"Did you enjoy it?"

"I enjoy every moment with your sexy ass," he replied. He finished getting dressed, then leaned over and gave her a passionate kiss. Kreasha tried to pull him back on the bed, but he stepped back. "I have to get back to the block and make sure everything is straight. When

I get back though, make sure you're ready," he said, walking out of the room.

"I will be," she purred, sticking a finger inside her pussy.

Justice headed back to the block he left the young bull watching, to make sure everything was okay. Chris still hadn't arrived, and he wasn't answering his cellphone. Justice knew it wasn't like Chris and hoped he hadn't gotten pinched.

As he stepped out of his car, he noticed a bunch of long faces. Not paying much attention to it, he continued walking toward his workers. Just as he was getting closer, he noticed the dude he had seen Gina with at the Chinese store. Later on he had found out his name was Ice, and he had the dope game on smash. He was standing across the street in the middle of a huddle as if he was holding a meeting. Justice grabbed a crate and took a seat. "What's good?"

Everyone was acting like he hadn't said a word.

"What's good?" He repeated again, thinking they didn't hear him the first time. As he sat there, one kid walked away. Shortly after, the other three workers walked away as well, leaving him there alone. Feeling a great deal of tension, Justice wondered what was going on. While he was trying to figure it out, he watched Ice and his crew, who were all watching him. A couple of minutes later, Justice's workers headed back toward him. One by one, they all dropped their work onto his lap.

Justice sat there with a look of confusion on his face. "What's up?" he asked.

"Ice said to give the work back," one of the young bulls mumbled.

"He said what?" Justice asked while switching his eyes over to Ice and his squad, who were all acting as if nothing was going on.

"He said to tell you that you were only out here on the strength of Malik, and being as though he's gone, you have to go."

"On the strength of Malik?" he repeated arrogantly and in disbelief. "I'm out here on the strength of me. I'm my own fucking man!" Justice wanted to straighten this out, but he realized now was not the time for it. Not when you're sitting on a block with over 250 bags of heroin sitting in your lap.

"I'm sorry boss," the other bull blurted out.

"Ha, ha," Justice laughed. "Okay, we'll see about this." Feeling totally disrespected, he quickly stood up and walked away furiously. He looked across the street at Ice, who was standing there looking directly at him.

This made Justice even more furious. He couldn't believe they were actually trying to run him off the block. His fear of getting arrested told him to leave, but his ego was begging him to stay. He shook his head from side to side with a devilish smirk on his face.

"You got that," he mumbled under his breath as he got into his car and pulled off.

He hoped Ice didn't think it was that simple. There was no way in the world Justice's huge ego would allow him to be run away from anywhere. He promised himself Ice would regret the fact that he attempted to disrespect him like this. A war had just begun, and Ice was the enemy.

CHAPTER 4

A couple days later Justice was standing on the sidewalk, surrounded by a crowd of customers copping dope from him. They all waited impatiently as he handed several bags of Lucifer to them one by one. Despite the orders he was given, he refused to allow Ice to run him away from the block. He had way too much pride for that. He wouldn't let Ice, or anyone else, for that matter, stand in the way of his money. Maybe if Ice had told him this a few months ago he would have had a better chance. It was way too late now though. Justice was already seeing the potential of getting rich off that block, and no one was going to mess that up. He had cut Chris off because Chris thought pussy was more important than money. Until he found a few soldiers that weren't scared to hold the block down, he would oversee it.

Hours passed and Justice continued serving

customer after customer while the group of young bulls watched with jealousy from across the street. The fact that he has a better quality of dope attracted the majority of the customers to him. Out of ten sales, nine came his way. Deep down inside, his competition wanted to join him, but their fear of Ice made them stay on that side struggling.

On the opposite side of the street, the young bulls were so eager to finish their packages, they were damn near fighting over who got the next sale that came in their direction. They were attacking the fiends like vultures, meeting them in the middle of the street, hoping they could make the sale before the fiends realized Justice was also out there. Some of them even posted up in the middle of the block, trying to cut potential customers' cars off, almost getting hit in the process just to make a sale. Lucifer was living up to its name, because people were heading straight to hell once trying it.

About $3,000 and an hour later, Ice pulled up on the scene, looking too calm for Justice.

“I hope you don’t start your bullshit,” Justice mumbled to himself.

Ice’s presence made Justice feel uneasy, even though he knew his .40 cal. was right on the driver’s seat of his car. He continued to act nonchalantly, trying to make Ice feel as if he was not paying him any attention at all. From the looks of it, Ice wasn’t paying him much attention either.

Each time Justice peeked across the street, Ice appeared to be doing his own thing. He was standing in the center of the crowd, talking really loudly, steadily amusing the guys around him.

Justice figured Ice would react like this. He felt the only reason he pulled that stunt was to try and scare him away, but it wasn’t going to work. Justice could tell Ice had no heart, but his money gave him a sense of power. The average guy was usually scared to go up against Ice and his team, but not Justice. He lived for violence and didn't mind getting his hands dirty.

Justice didn't care what Ice's game was, as long as it didn't affect him. If they crossed paths, Justice was surely going to expose him in front of the world. Suddenly a crowd of clients swarmed Justice all at once.

"Lucifer, who wants to try the best?" Justice yelled out to them.

As they approached him, he dug his hands deep down inside of his pants. From the seat of his boxers, he retrieved a plastic sandwich bag full of heroin packets.

"Can I get a bundle?" one fiend begged.

"Give me three!" shouted a female's voice.

"I'll take a brick!" another man demanded.

Justice took care of every order as they approached. He peeked around nervously, trying to watch out for police that may try to sneak up on him. Finally, the crowd dispersed. In a matter of minutes, Justice ran through almost a hundred bags. The money came so fast, he didn't even get a chance to count it. He couldn't wait to tell Supreme how much he had the block chirping now. This would be one of their most trusted blocks.

"Let's get this fucking money," he smiled to himself.

He took one more glance around the area before fixing his eyes on the sloppy knot of money he held in his hands. Then, bill by bill, he placed each one face up in the same direction so he could count it.

"Yizzo!" a voice said sternly, startling him.

Justice looked up quickly. He was shocked to see Ice stepping onto the curb along with another man he had never seen before. A slight bit of nervousness entered his body because he didn't have his burner on him. He regretted not retrieving it when he first saw them pull up, out of fear of the law.

"Yo, homie, what did I tell you the other day?" Ice asked, rapidly approaching Justice. "Malik ain't out here anymore, so you need to step also."

As they got within ten feet from Justice, they split up on opposite sides of him. Justice already peeped the blitz, and prepared himself for what was to come.

"So you needed help to come at me, you fucking coward," Justice said, not backing down. "I don't need anybody's permission to pump on this block. It's because of me it's doing these numbers."

He stepped backward, positioning himself so neither one of them could get the drop on him. As he was backpedaling, he stuffed his money into his pockets.

"A hard head makes a soft ass," Ice said sarcastically.

"Pssst," Justice sucked his teeth.

"Pssst what, nigga? What?" the dude that came with Ice said aggressively as he got within arm's reach of Justice.

Justice prepared himself to rumble, hoping they were not strapped, because he would be defenseless against them. He felt some type of way because he was about to rumble two grown-ass men. He hoped he hadn't bitten off more than he could chew. Now was not the time to debate though.

"What y'all trying to do, then?" he replied, already in go mode.

Crack! The quick blow landed on the man's cheekbone, catching him totally by surprise. The impact caused him to stumble backward, almost falling to the ground.

Justice quickly fired another two piece. Surprisingly, it landed on the man's chin bone, causing him to hit the ground hard. Justice looked back and forth, making sure he kept both of them in his eyesight. The dude quickly regained his composure and jumped back up. His eyes was full of rage as he tried to charge at Justice. Justice side stepped the charge, then punched the guy in the back of his head, causing him to stumble again. The man felt humiliated, just thinking a teenager was getting out on him. It made him feel disrespected.

As he came close, Ice inched closer as deviously as he could, but Justice peeped him. He wanted Ice so badly he could taste it. He stood there, feet planted, with his fists clenched tightly. His eyes switched from side to side. The guys were moving in on him. He realized he had to react fast or they would get on the inside. Justice locked eyes with the man to his left. He sensed fear and assumed the earlier punches had an effect on him.

Justice's assumption was correct. The man hesitated to run in on him because he would hate to get hit with another one of Justice's leg-wobbling blows. Justice jumped at him, faking him out as if he was about to swing again. He did this to buy himself some time. Just like he calculated, the dude backed up with fear. Justice then rushed to his right, going straight at Ice. With his elbow held high, he ran full speed at Ice. Ice's eyes lit up with fear. Justice gripped him by the collar, pulling him close, and smashed his elbow dead into Ice's face.

Ice grabbed his nose in a tremendous amount of pain.

Hoping that would hold Ice long enough for him to concentrate on the other guy, Justice rushed over to the other guy. They immediately squared off toe to toe. Justice felt extra confident he wouldn't lose to them, and was prepared to swing, when the dude rushed him. The impact of the right hand reached Justice before the man did. Although the blow was painful, Justice still managed to fire two wild haymakers to keep him away.

Justice was so caught up in the mix, he didn't even notice the aluminum-bat-toting man sneaking up behind him. Just as the man got close to him, Justice's senses told him to turn around, but it was already too late.

SMACK! The sound echoed as the bat greeted Justice's face, causing him to go down on one knee as stars appeared before his eyes. Everything became one big blur, and the street began to spin around. His head felt heavy, and the smell of blood filled his nostrils. He tried to shake the stars away to regain his composure.

Just as he was getting his self together, another blow came crashing down on top of his head, chopping him down like a tree.

"You fucked up, little boy!" the dude with Ice shouted sternly. Another blow sent Justice falling flat on his stomach. His face banged onto the concrete. "We're grown-ass men. I'ma teach you to stay in a child's place."

They started brutally stomping Justice, who was now balled up in the fetal position. Ice grabbed him by his collar, ripping it from his neck. The men then grabbed his pants legs and pulled them until they were completely off. Justice's boots came off in the midst of the struggle, leaving him with only his socks and boxers on. Fearing for his life, he lifted his head up. All he could see was a Timberland boot coming directly toward his head. He quickly grabbed hold of Ice's boot to prevent the kick from having a major impact. Holding onto the other man's pants leg, Justice managed to pull himself back onto one knee.

The painful kicks to his ribcage and back from the other two men were unbearable, but somehow he managed to get to his feet. He stood up, only to be greeted by a chrome handgun aimed directly at his head. His heart skipped a beat. He promised himself if he got out of this alive, he would never go anywhere else without his strap. Fear set in causing him to forget about the pain. Not even realizing it, Justice backhanded the gun out of the man's hand to prevent himself from being shot.

Boc! The gun went off when it hit the ground.

Justice ducked his head low and took off into flight. As he attempted to pass by, Ice tried to trip him with a sweeping motion of his foot. It knocked him slightly off balance, but the fear of getting shot made him keep stepping.

Boc! Boc! Boc! The gunfire sounded off repeatedly as Ice's partner snatched the gun off the ground and let it spark.

Justice lowered his body close to the ground and continued running as fast as he could. He dashed off of the curb and headed up the middle of the street. He hated the police, but wished one would ride past now to get those niggas off his ass. If only he could get to his car, he thought as he ran up the block.

Boc! Boc! The sound echoed again making Justice run faster, weaving in and out of parked cars.

A few blocks away, Bub was hunched back in the passenger seat of some chick's car, smoking a Dutch filled with loud. They cruised down the block listening to the Amigos, trying to find a spot so he could get some head, and maybe even more.

"Let me get some before you take that shit to the head," the chick said, reaching for the Dutch.

He handed it over and placed his hand between her legs, rubbing her pussy over the tight jeans she was wearing.

“Stop!” She playfully smacked his hand away.

As they approached the stop sign, Bub heard the sound of rapid gunfire. He leaned up to see where it was coming from.

“What the?” he blurted out.

The first thing he saw was some man firing recklessly behind a close to naked person, who was running for his life, trying to get away. Bub stared as they passed the gunman. When they passed the kid trying to escape, Bub looked back. He was shocked to see that underneath the bloody mess was his homie Justice.

“Yo, stop this muthafuckin car,” he yelled, pulling out his chrome .40 cal.

“Are you crazy?” the chick replied in a high-pitched voice.

“Stop this car! That’s my man out there.”

The chick continued to drive down the street out of fear of getting shot, totally disregarding what Bub just said. He snatched the steering wheel toward him, causing the car to swerve to the right. The girl slammed on the brakes and Bub jumped out, leaving the door open, letting the cannon roar.

Boom! Boom! Boom! Boom!

Ice and his two friends immediately took cover behind a parked car. Justice ran straight past the car at first. He was so busy dodging bullets, he didn't even notice who it was trying to save his life.

"Just, get in the car," Bub yelled.

He recognized the voice and looked back. When he saw Bub shooting at Ice, he was relieved. He rushed over to the car, and hopped in the backseat.

"Go!" Bub yelled to the scared girl in the driver's seat as he dove back in. She pulled off recklessly, with the door still wide open.

Boc! Boc! Boc! The gunfire sounded off from afar.

"Damn, nigga, what the fuck happened to you?" Bub asked curiously as he looked Justice over. He wasn't sure if Justice was hit or not. "You bleeding. Is you hit?"

Justice doesn't reply with words. Not because he didn't want to, but because the lump in his throat made it hard for him to speak. He just shook his head negatively. He was totally embarrassed Bub and his bitch had to see him like this. In his heart lay an abundance of rage.

"Let me see your phone," he said to Bub. He needed to call his brother and let him know what was going on. He couldn't believe what had just happened.

Bub had a smirk on his face thinking how he could have easily let those niggas murk Justice, but he decided to use the situation to his advantage. He still was going to get them back for what they did to his girl, but first he needed them to trust him. As Justice sat in the backseat, he replayed the situation in his head, already planning his retaliation.

CHAPTER 5

The sun was shining brightly on the glistening silver SLS Mercedes that just parked in front of the University of Delaware. It had gulf wing doors that opened up like eagle wings. The huge chrome wheels were damn near blinding. Everyone stood around admiring the vehicle. It was almost too beautiful to be on the streets. It looked like it belonged in a car show somewhere.

The vehicle was not foreign to the spectators because it pulled up faithfully every day at the exact same time. They all knew who the car was coming to pick up, but had no idea of who the driver was. He couldn't be seen on account of the dark tinted windows.

Minutes later, the beautiful freshman walked toward the Mercedes. No man in his right mind would ever believe she was only a freshman in college. She actually had to wait to attend college because of her financial situation. Her tight-fitting Seven jeans were glued to her protruding hips and curvy butt. Her 36Bs ripped through her tight T-shirt, with her nipples peeking vibrantly through like high beams as she exploited them proudly.

All the other students stopped just to watch her pass by. Once she finally made it to the car, she opened the door and lowered herself into the passenger seat. As she got in, her low-cut hip-huggers slid down extremely low, revealing two inches of crack for her audience. She and the driver traded a passionate kiss before he pulled off.

"I got something for you, sexy lady," he whispered. "Look in the backseat and see what it is."

She reached behind the seat and pulled out the Chanel shopping bag. Just seeing those double Cs excited her instantly. She couldn't wait to find out what surprise was waiting inside the bag. She prayed it was what she thought it was. She ripped through the wrapping paper like a child on Christmas day. What she found was the gift she had been wanting for quite some time now.

It was the pocketbook that matched the sneakers he gave her last week. She stared at the bag and couldn't help but think about all the compliments she was going to get. She hadn't seen anyone in her school with that bag yet. Matter of fact, she didn't think anyone in America owned one yet. She ordered it several months ago, and she finally had it in her possession.

She was so joyful, she damn near dove into his lap, squeezing his neck tightly, disregarding the fact that he was driving. He peeked over at her, and the look of happiness he saw, made him gloat excessively.

"Thank you, baby," she shouted.

"That's nothing, ma," he replied arrogantly. "Tell me I don't take care of my baby girl! You're the first one in your school with that bag. Bitches gonna be hating on you!"

"Is they?" she agreed cheerfully. She blushed

continuously as she examined every stitch of the bag.

She was by far one of the baddest chicks at UD. Some of the clothes and accessories she wore, other students and teachers could only dream of owning. Not one day passed that she didn't count her blessings. She considered herself extremely lucky to have a boyfriend who luxuriated her lifestyle in such a manner. Just a few years ago, she was considered one of the less fortunate students.

A closet full of Gap and Old Navy was all she owned. Any article of clothing that was of any value was a hand-me-down from her older cousin. Puberty was the best thing that could have ever happened to her. Her voluptuous behind and firm breasts were the best present God could have given her, in her eyes. For years she complained about her figure and prayed she would someday develop like the models she saw on television.

It seemed like it all happened overnight. She went from a little, dirty, flat-chested nerd, to Kreasha, the most popular girl in school. She couldn't believe all the attention the boys gave her. It made her feel very special.

When she would walk to the store, she'd return with at least five phone numbers. None of the numbers even mattered to her until she met Supreme. It was love at first sight for both of them, and even though she was older than he was, it didn't matter. She had thought she would turn him out, but it eventually turned out to be the other way around. The two of them had been together when he wasn't getting money, so it was only right that he showed his appreciation now that he was up.

"How happy are you?" he asked.

"Very happy!"

"Oh yeah? Well make me as happy as you are," he whispered with a devilish smirk on his face.

"Uhhmm," she uttered, knowing exactly what it took to make him happy, "I wonder what I can do?"

She looked him dead in the eyes while extending her

left hand onto his lap. In a matter of seconds, she had his pants unzipped. His manhood peeked attentively through the slit of his boxers. Kreasha leaned her head onto his lap and went to work. The sound of her slurping on his erection overpowered the sound of the music coming through the speakers.

He lay low in the seat, just enjoying her mouth as he cruised down the road. The level of ecstasy she was taking him to made it difficult for him to concentrate on driving. Not even a half a block and he already had the urge to release his load. She was the best at giving head, and he never got enough of it.

"Aghh," he grunted as he exploded, gently palming the back of her head. She didn't budge until he released every drop into her mouth.

Coincidentally, they finished just as he pulled in front of her house. She lifted her head up and looked into his half-closed eyes.

"Are you happy now?"

"You already know," he laughed. "Damn, ma, you're the best."

"Get yourself together," she teased, grabbing hold of her bags.

"Bring that out to me, sexy," he said as she opened the door to get out.

"All of it?" she asked, peeking around to see who was watching.

"Yeah, all of it."

Kreasha jumped out and ran into the house. In a matter of minutes, she returned carrying a large duffle bag in her hand. She ran to the driver's side and dropped the bag through the window, onto his lap.

"Thanks, baby! I will see you tonight, right?"

"I have an exam tomorrow, but maybe afterward."

"Come on, I'll bring you back home early so you can get your beauty rest. I wish you would just stay with me," he said.

She looked him in the eyes, knowing he knew

exactly how to get to her. Seeing him beg had always been her weakness. It was so hard for her to tell him no. She realized how much he had changed her life, and the last thing she wanted to do was make him think she was not grateful. She would hate to piss him off and run him away from her. At this point she couldn't imagine life without him.

"Okay, but I have to be back early."

"I'll pick you up soon as I take care of this run," he said, giving her a kiss. Just as he was about to pull off, his phone started ringing. "Yo, what's up?"

"Yo, Preme, some niggas just shot at me," Justice yelled over the line.

"Where you at?"

"I'm at Gabby's crib. Meet me there."

"En route!" he replied, ending the call. He turned to Kreasha, who was waiting patiently. "We're gonna have to postpone . Someone just came at my brother."

"Be careful, Preme," was all she was able to get out.

Sccuuurr, the tires screeched as they gripped the pavement. Someone had tried to hurt his brother, so therefore they had tried to hurt him. Now it was on and popping.

~ ~ ~

It was now ten o'clock at night, and Supreme, Justice, Bub, and Tank were riding around in a stolen SUV, in search of Ice and his friends. Justice still couldn't get over the fact that they had tried to play him. In fact, they totally humiliated him, beating him out of his clothes in front of everyone like he was a child.

Even if he wanted to let it go, he couldn't. His ego would never allow him to do such a thing. A stunt like that could cause everyone to think he was sweet, and try to disrespect him too. It was bad enough that his own workers were scared.

"We've been riding around for hours, man, and there's still no sign of bull," Bub said, turning up Ice's block once again.

Justice realized he had to do something to bring Ice out of hibernation. He sat in the backseat thinking about his next move. In his lap lay a sixteen-shot Heckle and Koch .40 cal. handgun. It was fully loaded and ready to rip. Supreme was holding a .44 Magnum in his hand, while Tank was gripping a riot pump. Bub pulled into the first available parking spot. From there they could see everything going on.

"Look at how those fiends are swarming the block. That should be my shit out there," Justice mumbled, becoming jealous.

The sight of Ice making money only infuriated him. He looked closely in search of Ice, but knew it was unlikely he would show up.

"The only way to bring that nigga out is to hit him in his pockets," Supreme said with a smile.

"Let's do it," Tank replied, clicking the safety off the pump.

Justice waited for the right moment to catch

everyone standing together so they could hit them all at once. “Now!”

Bub zoomed out of the parking space in a hurry. The tires squealed as he mashed the gas. The smell of burning rubber filled the air instantly. They raced up the block, on the wrong side of the street. The hustlers were so busy making moves, they didn’t even notice the reckless SUV ripping up the block.

The SUV hopped the curb, damn near hitting everyone standing there. Bub slammed on the brakes, blocking the entrance to the alleyway, making it impossible for the hustlers to run and retrieve any of their weapons. Justice jumped out while the vehicle was still moving, followed by Supreme, with their weapons aimed at the young boys.

“If you’re not trying to die, get the fuck outta here,” Justice threatened, aiming his gun at the customers. They quickly dispersed from the area.

“Back the fuck up,” Supreme told the three young

boys. He forced them into the alleyway. He dug his hands into the first boy's pocket. "This ain't really got nothing to do with y'all. You're just in the way. You can blame this on your bitch-ass boss. Now empty your pockets."

They all begin pulling huge knots of money from their pockets. Supreme grabbed the money from them and threw it in a brown shopping bag that had been in one of the trashcans. "You take me to the stash," he said, placing the nose of the gun to the boy's neck.

"Huh?"

"You heard me, motherfucker. I want it all," Justice said.

He knew the routine. Ice kept bricks of dope on reserve, so he didn't have to make any drop-offs throughout the day. The boy hesitated until Justice placed the gun against his right temple. The look in his eyes reassured the boy he meant business.

"It's over there!" he said, pointing to an area of the

alley.

"Y'all lay down on the ground," Supreme told the other two.

"Hurry the fuck up," Justice instructed him.

The boy stepped up his pace and galloped to the opening of a yard. Once they were in the yard, the boy bent down and sifted through a pile of garbage with his hands. Finally, he retrieved a shopping bag, then handed it to Justice without hesitation.

"Is this all of it?" he stated, fumbling through the bag. "If I look through this garbage and find more, I'm going to leave your ass back here stinking."

"That's all of it," the boy stuttered.

Justice counted seventeen bricks in the bag. He then trotted out of the yard, almost dragging the boy behind him. When he reached the entrance where his brother was, he pushed the boy to the ground.

"Y'all niggas tell Ice, if I can't eat out here, nobody gon eat. Tell him I said he's gonna get dealt with when

I see him."

What he did next made everyone's stomach turn. He threw all the money and dope in a trash can, then lit it on fire. Tank and Bub both stared at each other in disbelief. They thought they were going to split everything up.

"What the hell you do that for?" Tank asked.

"Like I said, this is only the beginning." He looked over at the young boys. "Choose sides. Y'all better get with the A-team, 'cause there won't be no B-team. It's going to go down like this every day until that nigga shows his face. I'm warning y'all to stay out of my way. I don't have any beef with y'all, only that pussy. Anybody I see out here pumping from now on is on Ice's side and will be dealt with accordingly. The next time, it's gonna be bloodshed."

They all jumped in the SUV and Bub bounced off the sidewalk. Supreme liked the way his brother handled the whole situation.

Boc! Boc! Boc! Tank fired three warning shots in the air.

When they got back to Supreme's car, he and Justice hopped in and headed to the crib so they could prepare for what was about to come. Justice told Tank to get rid of the stolen vehicle.

"I'm gonna go with you," Bub told Tank. "We need to talk."

CHAPTER 6

Even though they didn't put anything on the block Ice had, there was still plenty of money being made in other areas. They had the whole city on smash, and nobody made money without them being involved. Everybody wanted to get what Supreme and Justice were selling. If the baggies didn't have the name Lucifer on them, the fiends didn't cop from them. They were hurting all the other dealers' pockets, and they enjoyed it.

"And we lie together, cry together. And I swear I hope we fucking die together. And I'll be loving you forever. You're all I need to get by . . ." Dej Loaf and Rick Ross blared through the speakers.

Justice was leaned back in the passenger seat as Gabby cruised down the street in the new car he just copped off the lot. It was a cherry-red convertible Maybach.

"I used to play hard to get, like a sample on a hook. We used to play with pots, you told me you was a cook. I was runnin' too long, he was chasing, didn't trip. How'd he do it? I don't know, but somehow I got hooked. Thug passion, he so compassionate. MMG, yeah, that's his acronym. Call him D-A-D-D-Y like I'm in a bassinet . . ."

"Turn that down some," Justice said, sparking the Dutch.

Gabby was so happy to be in her new ride, she didn't hear him. She was showing off for all the hating-ass bitches that stared at them as they rode past. Justice leaned up and turned the music down.

"Why you do that?" she whined.

"I'm not trying to get pulled over while I'm strapped. Look at all those cop cars up there. This shiny ass car is going to bring too much attention. That's why I said you should have chose the black or white one instead."

"But I like this one," she replied, pouting her lips.

Justice laughed because she knew that soft shit didn't work on him. He only bought the car for her because it was her birthday. He wanted every nigga in the hood to know who she belonged to.

"I have something else to show you tomorrow, but tonight we're going out to celebrate your day."

Gabby was excited about everything he was doing for her. She still remembered how she helped him that day after school when he was getting jumped by a couple of bullies. Then when they finally talked at his birthday party. Ever since that day, they had been a couple. Justice was going to ask her to move in together tomorrow. That was the big surprise he had been waiting to throw her way.

"We can't tonight, popi. We are going to Puerto Rico to see my grandma. She is very sick, and they don't know how long she has left."

"That's more important, so go handle that, and I'll

see you when you get back," Justice said, giving her a kiss. "Drop me off at my car."

"I'm going to leave this parked in the garage, so you don't have to worry, okay?"

"I'm not, now turn your music back up and let muthafuckas keep hating on you," he smirked as he leaned back in his seat.

Gabby loved her car and was mad she wouldn't be able to show off to everybody until she returned. For now though, she was the baddest bitch around. She put her sunglasses on and cranked the volume as they headed to Justice's car: "Let the dog roam, he found his way back. Loyal to the soil, I never change that. We go way back, I can take you way back. Use to ride Chevys only, now we're in a Maybach, yeah."

~ ~ ~

Ice and his worker Fatboy were parked in the Food Lion parking lot talking about what happened with his shit.

"Yeah, I took a hell of a loss," he informed Fatboy. "But I'm a bounce right back. I'm a fucking hustler."

Fatboy just sat there quietly, looking straight ahead.

"I just want to know which one of them niggas showed them where my shit was. I will get to the bottom of that shit though. That is what I pay you for, and here it is I'm the one that has to fix this."

"I can take care of it, Ice. I already called for a meeting later on after we finish our business," Fatboy replied.

Fatboy was trying to play it cool, but he was nervous as hell. He prayed Ice never found out he was the one who showed them where the work was. He tried extra hard to keep a baffled look on his face, just to throw Ice off. He really felt terrible that he gave up the stash, but he wasn't trying to die. Ice had always been good to him. They'd been getting money together for the past few years.

However, he knew if he hadn't told Supreme and

Justice what they wanted to know, he would have been somewhere stinking right now. He felt like he was in a no-win situation. Ice dropped the plastic bag onto Fatboy's lap.

"Let's make it happen. You go set up and I'ma park out here just in case those niggas try to come through." Ice sensed fear in Fayboy's eyes. "Don't worry, homie, we'll get everyone that had something to do with this."

Fatboy opened the door and hopped out hesitantly. He dashed through the alley quickly. Once he was out of Ice's view, he took a deep breath knowing he had gotten away with the lie. He ran all the way to the back of the yard to a huge pile of rubbish. He dug deep inside the stack of garbage and planted the bag inside. He then scattered the junk back on top to cover it. Just as he was about to stand up, he heard movement behind him.

Boom! A gun sounded off. The .357 slug crashed into the back of Fatboy's skull, sending him tumbling over into the pile of garbage face-first. Tank stood over him holding the smoking cannon in his hand. He snatched him up by the collar and flung him back to the ground. Fatboy landed on his back hard. In the center of his forehead, was a hole the size of a lemon. Crimson red covered his entire face. Tank looked closely to see if he was still breathing. Fatboy was still as could be, but Tank wanted to make sure.

Boom! Boom! Both shots ripped through Fatboy's forehead.

Tank hopped the fence, ran through the alley, and ended up on the back block where Bub had been standing as a lookout.

"Come on, let's get out of here," Bub said, as they both took off running.

Once they were out of the alley, they spotted the Chevy Impala sitting there waiting for them. Tank tucked his gun under his shirt before walking out. He jumped in the backseat while Bub sat in the front.

"You sure he's dead?" Ice asked nervously.

"Is I'm sure he dead?" Tank asked sarcastically. "I hit that motherfucker three times in the head at close range. You answer that question. I don't play games."

"How his face look when he saw you?" Bub asked.

"I didn't see his face. I crept up on him from behind."

"Awww, don't tell me you went out like that," Bub teased him, with a smile. "I know you didn't shoot the man from behind? That's some bullshit."

"Go ahead, nigga! I crept that nigga from behind because he got caught slipping. He was too busy bent over stashing what he thought was dope," he explained.

"You could at least let the man get up and look you in the eyes before you killed him. That was a cowardly stunt you pulled," he said. "You know the rules, never shoot a man in the back."

"I didn't shoot him in the back. I shot him in the head," Tank replied arrogantly.

"You know what the fuck I mean!"

"You already know where my gangsta at. I'll shoot a motherfucker in the head, face, back, and anywhere else. It doesn't matter to me as long as the nigga ain't breathing when I leave."

"Okay, okay!" Ice blurted out. "What fucked me up is, the lil nigga sat there acting like he didn't have a clue of who took my shit. That's crazy!"

"For sure!" they both said simultaneously, finally agreeing on something.

"Okay, so you proved you're trying to get down, but why?" Ice asked, suspicious.

"Those niggas killed both of our peeps, and we want to get them back for that shit," Bub said, feeling rage building up.

"Plus, ever since that nigga Preme came back into the picture, Justice been acting funny toward us," Tank chimed in.

"Sounds like jealousy to me, but whatever. Anyway, you have proven to be worthy adversaries, and I can definitely use you. If you take them niggas out, I will make both of you partners, and you can still control the areas you already have."

"Had!" Tank replied, knowing there was no turning back, now that they had made a deal with the devil.

"Well, you'll have them back again once the competition is eliminated. So do we have a deal?"

They all shook hands and went their separate ways before someone heard the shots and contacted the police.

CHAPTER 7

Supreme was locked in his room blasting the Amigos. The music was so loud that the bass was making the walls tremble. He jumped up from the floor after finishing his fiftieth set of pushups. He worked hard to stay in shape and keep his six pack. His braids had turned into dreads and were flowing freely down his back. He stood in the mirror, admiring what he saw.

He winked at himself before smiling, exposing his bright white teeth. He placed his hands on his hips while slightly twisting his torso, posing like a body builder. He tightened up his brick-hard abdomen exposing his beautiful eight pack. He then stretched his arms straight out and flexed his muscles. He was really feeling himself ever since he started working out. Women would comment on his abs whenever he would walk around with his shirt off. After his workout, Supreme was ready to get his eat on. He walked into the kitchen where Justice was already sitting at the table eating.

"There you go with that workout shit again. Give it a break, nigga," Justice mumbled.

"You just hating on me, bro," Supreme said as he flexed his muscles for his brother. "You better get with the program and workout with me bones."

"Fuck you, nigga," Justice shot back.

"Shots fired!" Kreasha said, walking in on the two of them. She walked over and sat on Supreme's lap, giving him a peck on the lips. "Justice you better leave my baby alone before we jump your ass up in this bitch."

"You're gonna need some more help to come at me. I'm a beast with these," he said, holding up his fist.

They all busted out laughing at the comment. Supreme stood up, grabbed a salad bowl, then poured himself a bowl of cereal. Kreasha and Justice watched as he picked up a mixing spoon and sat at the table.

"Look at his greedy ass. Why don't you ever eat like a normal person?" Justice mumbled.

"It takes too long," Supreme told him.

"You're just greedy," Justice said. "We have to go look at that place, so can you hurry up and get dressed?"

"Let me take a shower real quick," Supreme said, getting up from the table. "Just give me about twenty minutes."

Justice went in the living room and sat on the couch. Kreasha came behind him with a Dutch in hand. She sat down, sparked it up, then took a couple of puffs before offering it to Justice. He took a few pulls, then passed it back.

"That shit right there is fire."

"I know! My homegirl fucks with some dude that gets a lot at one time," Kreasha replied, leaning back in her seat.

Justice couldn't help but stare under her skirt. She had her legs cocked open and wasn't wearing any panties. When she realized what he was staring at, she closed them. He just smiled at her quick reaction, then got up to grab his phone. He wanted to confirm their appointment with the realtor and let her know they were running a bit behind. Once he got off the phone, he reached for the Dutch Kreasha had hanging from her mouth.

"Let me get that," he said, pulling it from between her lips.

"Stop playing," she said, playfully punching him in the leg.

He tried to back away from her, but she grabbed the front of his pants causing him to stumble forward. He landed right between her legs. She could feel his manhood rising and her kitty starting to tingle. They both could feel the chemistry between them, and immediately pulled away. Kreasha was thinking how much he and Supreme looked alike. The fact that they were identical twins only made it that much easier to make the mistake she almost made.

"Give me my shit back and roll your own," Kreasha

smirked at him.

“Bet!” Justice said, giving her the Dutch back.

They heard Supreme coming down the steps. Kreasha crossed her legs so he didn’t see her not wearing panties, and get suspicious.

“Come on, bro, we have to seal the deal before someone else tries to.”

“Right behind you,” Justice replied, finishing up rolling the Dutch.

“You gonna stay here, or you want to tag along with us?” Supreme asked Kreasha.

“I’ll stay here and wait for Melissa to come. We’re going to Christiana Mall to pick up something to wear for the party.”

“A’ight!” Supreme said walking out the door. Him and Justice hopped in the car, heading to meet the realtor.

Supreme was reclined in the passenger seat, puffing on the loud Justice had gotten from Kreasha. The windows were up with the AC blowing. As they cruised down Market Street, Justice's attention was stolen by two of the prettiest girls he'd ever seen in his life.

"Goddamn!" he shouted.

"What?" Supreme asked, looking around.

"Them two bitches over there. Look at that ass," he said, licking his lips.

"Man, fuck them bitches right now. We have shit to do, bro!"

Justice disregarded Supreme's remarks and decided to stop anyway. He peeked around before busting a reckless U-turn in the middle of the street. The sounds of heavy horn blowing from the oncoming traffic caused Supreme to sit up.

"Just, you're fucking crazy. You trying to kill us for them raggedy-ass bitches."

"Nigga, you can say what you want. Shorty's ass is crazy." He pulled alongside them as they were walking. Neither of them acted as if they noticed him pull up.

Justice rolled the window down to get their attention. "Excuse me!"

Neither of them acknowledged him calling them. They just kept moving, not even looking in his direction.

Supreme was getting angry. "Man, fuck that bitch!" he shouted furiously. "She hears you calling her."

"Shorty!"

"What?" she finally answered. "Can't you see I'm not interested?" she asked. "I like the same thing you like."

"And what's that?"

"Pussy, motherfucker!"

"Yo, ma, watch your mouth."

"Pssst," she sucked her teeth. "Watch my mouth? Please! Who the fuck is you? Fuck you!"

"Fuck you too, bitch!"

"Your mother is a bitch," she yelled as they stepped off the curb into the intersection. As she was crossing the street, Justice stopped the car directly in front of them, cutting them off.

“Move, you stupid motherfucker.”

Supreme had a cup in the cup holder filled with the strawberry milkshake he bought earlier that day. Justice snatched the cup and tossed it at her. The shake splattered all over her face and blouse. She stood there in total shock.

“Shut the fuck up, you stupid-ass bitch!” He laughed as he pulled off, leaving her standing there embarrassed, and stupid.

“Oh shit, you’re fucking crazy!” Supreme said, laughing so hard tears began pouring down his face.

“Fuck that bitch. She got what she deserved. Nobody disrespects our mom and gets away with it,” he replied while Supreme continued to cheer him on.

At the corner, they stopped at the intersection for the red light. A white Chevy Impala squeezed into the little space between them and the curb. Both Supreme and Justice were so busy laughing, they didn’t even notice the car's presence. Supreme finally stopped laughing long enough to notice the vehicle. He quickly peeked to his right. First, he spotted a familiar face in the passenger's seat. Then he spotted a chrome 9mm aimed his way. It was Ice!

BOC! BOC! BOC!

"Go, Just!" Supreme shouted, ducking down.

Justice accelerated, attempting to get away, but the Impala was glued to their side. Supreme could see the smile on Ice's face. The driver had his right hand glued to the steering wheel while his left hand gripped the 9mm. He squeezed again trying to hit Supreme, but missed everything due to the fact that he couldn't aim while driving. Supreme finally got ahold of his gun. He switched the safety off and fired back without aiming.

BOOM! BOOM! BOOM! BOOM!

He just wanted to send some shots back hoping to get them off their ass. It worked, as the driver swerved, ducking the shots.

BOC! BOC!

Justice realized it was getting way too heated. It was time for him to use his expert driving skills. The cars continued racing up the block side by side while exchanging heavy gunfire with each other. Suddenly Supreme aimed at the driver side wheels and let off two precise shots, hitting Ice's back tire. Their car swerved out of control, running into a parked car. Justice slammed on the brakes and was about to back up, when they heard an army of sirens rapidly approaching.

"Let's go, bro," Supreme shouted.

He drove a few blocks then pulled over trying to calm their adrenaline. They sat quietly in shock for a matter of seconds. They realized how close they had been to losing their lives.

"You cool, Preme?"

"Yeah, did you see that faggot-ass nigga Ice in the passenger seat laughing?"

"Don't worry, he's gonna get his for sure. I'm going

to personally park that nigga for good when I catch him," Justice replied.

"You know it. We definitely have to get that crib now and get away from this area."

"Well call her and tell her we're on 95 now," Justice said, heading for the highway. "And I have to get rid of this car while we're out."

"Cool!" was Supreme's only response as he tucked his gun under the seat and relaxed, trying to collect his thoughts.

CHAPTER 8

Dominique and Donte drove through South Philly sipping on Hennessy. They were trying to finish up collecting the money from all their spots. They were so busy drinking and counting their share of the money, they hadn't noticed the Grand Marquis that had been following them since they left their Chester spots. Dom slowed down and turned into the gas station on Passyunk Avenue to get some gas before they hit the highway back to Delaware.

Soon as Dom pulled up to the gas pump, a couple of kids ran up to the car offering to pump their gas. Donte passed one of the kids a fifty-dollar bill, then told him to fill it up, and keep the change. The kid ran inside to pay for the gas while the other one snatched the nozzle from the pump and inserted it into the gas tank.

"I'm going inside to get something to drink. You want something?" Donte asked.

"Yeah, get me an Arizona ice tea," Dom said, rolling up the loud for their trip. "I need something to wash these Motrins down."

When Donte walked into the store, Dom noticed the Marquis pulling into the station. It wasn't the car that piqued her interest, but who was inside. She wondered what they were doing in Philly. She thought maybe they were about to go visit somebody. Donte walked out of the store just as they were opening the car door. He saw them, and just as he was about to speak, Bub fired a few shots, causing Donte to drop the bag he was carrying.

POP! POP! POP!

Dominique sat there in total shock without having a clue of what was going on. The shots were coming so fast, she didn't have time to react. Bub quickly fired again, this time hitting Donte twice in the leg and once in the shoulder. Donte grabbed at his shoulder, before falling backward to the ground. The two kids and a couple of bystanders that were standing around took off searching for cover. Dom reached in the glove box for her gun.

BOCA! BOCA!BOCA!

She let off three shots to get their attention off of Donte. He jumped up and ran for the car. The element of surprise caught them off guard and they ducked down. Once Donte was in the car, Dom hit the gas pedal and sped off with the nozzle still inside the gas tank.

POP! POP!

Bub fired as Tank pulled away. They headed in the opposite direction, trying to get away from the scene.

"I got his stupid ass! I should have shot his bitch too! That's who I really wanted anyway," Bub stated. "Little dumb motherfucker."

"I think you hit him in the chest," Tank said. "Before he fell, he grabbed his chest."

"I tried to take his fucking head off," Bub replied, sounding disappointed by the results. "It don't matter, he's probably dead by now anyway."

~ ~ ~

Dom raced down the street doing about a hundred

miles per hour, with the passenger's door still half open, trying to get as far away as possible.

"Aghhh, my fucking shoulder. I'm hit," he whined. "I need to get to a hospital."

Dom drove faster worrying about her man. She kept checking her mirror to make sure she wasn't being followed.

"What the fuck was Tank and Bub shooting at us for?" Dominique asked. "You think Supreme and Justice tried to off us?"

"Aghhh, no they wouldn't do this to us. Call them and let them know what happened."

"Where you hit at?"

"I think all of them hit me," he mumbled. "Sssss, ah, my chest is on fire."

Dom could see he was in a lot of pain. He was rolling around in the passenger seat trying to alleviate the pain. She made it to the University of Pennsylvania hospital in no time. He was damn near lying on the floor. The pain was unbearable as he continued to hold his chest.

"Yo!"

"Supreme, Donte was shot. We just arrived at University. It was Tank and that nigga Bub," she stated hysterically.

"What?" Supreme yelled in disbelief.

"They fucking shot him while we were at the gas station."

"Where he hit at?" Justice inquired nervously. "Is he alright?" Supreme had them on speaker phone so they both could hear what was going on.

"I don't know. He got hit like four or five times."

"Aghh, aghh!" Donte cried out interrupting Dom.

"You hear him?" she asked.

"Yo, we're on our way there right now. We were shot at too by that pussy-ass nigga Ice and one of his goons. It might be all tied in together," Supreme said. "Don't trust anyone right now, Dom, and keep your heat close just in case. We'll see you in a few minutes."

They first had to ditch the car they were in because

it was shot up. Justice stopped at a used car lot and gave it to them, along with three grand for a new vehicle. It was a 2007 Pontiac Grand Prix, supercharged. They needed something with speed, and that's exactly what they got.

Fear filled Justice's body as he thought of the fact that Donte has been hit. He wondered how serious it was. He also wondered what Tank and Bub had to do with this. Although he knew it could happen, he never thought it would be one of his close friends. Not to mention, one of their own crew who did the shooting. He even thought about how it could have easily been him or his twin that could have been sitting up in a hospital, clinging to their life. The thought sent chills up his spine. Now more than ever he realized just how dangerous this beef was, and that both teams wanted to come out on top.

~ ~ ~

When they arrived at the emergency room, Dominique parked at the front entrance.

"I can't go in with you right now," she said. "I have the gun on me, and I have to ditch this car somewhere first."

Donte knew once he went in there, the cops were going to be on his ass, asking all types of questions about who shot him.

"I'll get out here. Ditch this shit quickly," he moaned.

"Okay, I'll be back soon as I can," Dom replied, giving him a kiss.

Donte used all of his energy to push the door open. He sort of crawled out of the car, falling onto the pavement. The pain was so unbearable, he couldn't even lift himself from the ground. Dom was baffled about what she should do. She mashed the gas pedal a little, inching up a couple of feet.

"Help, help," Donte screamed out at the top of his lungs trying to get someone's attention. "I'm shot! Somebody help me!"

Dante's cries alarmed Dom, letting her know it was

time to go. She reached over and pulled the passenger door closed. Seconds later, doctors, nurses, and EMT workers flooded the entrance. That was Dom's cue to get the hell out of there. She was sure the police would be there soon, and they'd want some answers.

She stepped on the gas, racing out of the parking lot. As she was about to exit the grounds, she glanced in her rearview mirror and saw Donte being placed on a stretcher and rushed into the building. That whole ordeal had been too much for Dominique. She was shook up, but still on point for anything suspicious. She called Justice and told them where to meet her so they could figure out their next move. One thing for sure, she was going to get back at Tank and Bub for what they had done to her man.

CHAPTER 9

Supreme and Justice had just left the hospital from visiting Donte. He was in stable condition, but still in massive pain. He was so lucky to be alive. The shots to his shoulder, hip, and thigh were all minor compared to the chest wound. The bullet entered his chest, just barely one inch from his heart.

Justice was so thankful Donte didn't die. Now more than ever, he realized this beef had just taken a turn for the worst. Two people he called family were somehow siding with the enemy. What bothered him was, why? That's when it hit him: Bub was somehow related to the girl that was killed that time they jammed those out-of-town niggas. He should have said something to them and her life could have been spared. But what did Tank have to do with this?

Even though he second-guessed his actions, he knew it was too late. Now his only alternative was to turn the heat all the way up. Supreme rode shotgun while Justice cruised down one of Ice's blocks. They both learned a valuable lesson when they were in the enemy's territory: No more wearing their guns tucked in their waist. Both of them had their burners sitting on their laps.

As they rode, Justice was planning his next attack. Different ideas flowed through his head, but none seemed to stand out to him right away. There was one thing he was sure of, and that was, everybody that had anything to do with Ice was as good as dead. It was kill or be killed from here on out. He knew until the beef was over, they wouldn't be able to keep making money.

They would definitely need to keep their money game up, after the surprise he and Justice got for their women. They finally purchased the house of their dreams. It was a six-bedroom, two-and-a-half bathroom condo, with a four-car garage. The whole downstairs had glass walls, and the floors were covered with plush carpeting from wall to wall.

"Let's go get something to eat. I'm starving," Supreme stated.

"Me too!" Chris replied.

When Justice told Chris what had happened to them, he couldn't believe Tank would do that to them. As much as he loved Tank, he loved Justice even more. So there wasn't any hesitation when he had to pick a side.

They had just left the club on Broad and Erie, and decided to stop at Max's to get some food before heading home. While cruising down Germantown Avenue, in search of a parking spot, Supreme spotted the car that was chasing them the other day, parked on the side street. He thought his prayers had just been answered. Never did they expect to see Ice there.

"It's amazing that when you're not looking for someone, you find them," Justice said.

"Let me out. I got this nigga," Chris blurted out.

"You sure, bro?" Supreme asked.

"Yeah, I'm a get that motherfucker."

Chris hopped out of the car, then hid a few cars from where Ice car was parked. He waited patiently for him to come out. Omar walked slowly down the street, carrying his food in a plastic bag. As he got close to the car, he pressed the alarm button on his keyring to unlock the door. When he reached for the door handle, Chris jumped out from between the parked cars, holding an all-black .45. He wasn't expecting the driver to be Omar, but right now he would settle for whoever he could get.

Chris aimed his gun at Omar, ready to fire. Omar turned around just in the nick of time.

BOC!

Chris fired, hitting nothing at all. Omar had a shocked look on his face. In no way was he expecting to be shot at while coming from the store. He backpedaled away nervously.

BOC!

Chris fired again. Omar ducked down, attempting to make his way to the middle of the street, to buy some time. He moved to the opposite side of the car, dropping his food and snatching his gun from his waist. Chris noticed him drawing, and fired again trying to hit him before he get off a shot off.

BOC! Click! Click!

The constant squeezing of the trigger must have caused his gun to jam. He squeezed once again with the same result. Chris's heart dropped down to his boxers. He wished he would have let Supreme or Justice handle the situation instead. He was trying to show he had heart too, but it seemed to be backfiring right now.

Omar realized what was happening, and rushed in for the attack. He moved in with caution, just in case Chris managed to fire another shot. He squeezed the trigger as he moved in.

BOOM! BOOM!

Chris backed away from him, not realizing he had

trapped himself against a brick wall. Omar quickly approached him trying to get the drop.

Sccuuurrrr! Supreme and Justice stopped right in front of where Omar was standing. Supreme slammed on the brakes causing the Grand Prix's tires to make a loud noise. Justice fired from the passenger's seat trying to take Omar's wig off.

BOC! BOC! BOC!

Omar tumbled forward after the first shot. He rolled over and squeezed off two more times just to keep Justice off his ass. Justice in return aimed at him and squeezed three times consecutively. As they were shooting at each other, Chris hauled ass and jumped into the backseat. The sound of police sirens could be heard faintly. Seconds later, flashing lights appeared at the end of the block. They were coming full speed, straight at them. Two more cars were right behind the lead car.

"Go, go!" Justice shouted.

Supreme sped off in a hurry, peeking in his rearview

mirror. By now, the first police car was about a half a block away, and gaining. The second car joined in on the chase, while the third one stopped to secure the scene where Omar was still lying. Fear set in, causing Supreme to mash down on the gas. He wondered if his brother bodied the dude or not.

"Show me what kind of horsepower this bitch has," Justice shouted, fastening his seatbelt. Chris saw what was happening and followed suit.

Supreme raced through the streets recklessly, trying to ditch the police cars chasing behind them. As he approached the corner, he swerved the car from left to right purposely, attempting to confuse the cops about which way he was about to turn. When he faked to the left at the corner, the cops fell for the bait. Supreme was about to bend the corner, but then he cut the wheel to the right and made a full turn. That maneuver set the police back a few feet.

They spotted two cars parked on opposite corners at

the end of the block, waiting for them to come through. Supreme decided to make a quick right instead of going straight, onto Lehigh Avenue. In the distance, at least seven police cars could be seen in his rearview. When he made another left, he got the surprise of a lifetime. There were two cars parked nose to nose, setting up a roadblock to block them off.

“Holy shit! What the fuck are we gonna do now?” Chris asked.

Supreme just continued forward with no regard, heading straight for them. The officers showed no sign of fear. They hoped he would slow down once he saw them, but Supreme knew it was way too late to stop now. The officers ran for cover and ducked behind their cars. They pulled their weapons and held them up hoping to intimidate the drivers of the car from doing something stupid.

Just in the nick of time, right before striking the cruisers, Supreme cut the steering wheel to the right.

The Grand Prix jumped the curb and headed down the sidewalk.

BOC! BOC! BOC! BOC!

The shots from the officers' .40 calibers sounded off just as they passed them. The car rocked as two of the four shots found their target, shattering the back window. That made Supreme drive even faster down the sidewalk. He turned back on the street once they were clear of the roadblock.

"Get us out of here, bro."

"Shut up, nigga, I'm trying," Supreme replied. He peeked around nervously, looking for any escape route. Suddenly he saw the expressway sign up ahead.

"Hurry up, Preme! They're still coming," Justice replied.

Supreme checked his mirror again to see how much of a lead he had on them. To his surprise he saw about ten to fifteen cars trailing way behind them. He was confident there was no way possible they'd be able to catch up with him. He quickly jumped onto I-76 and sped down the expressway doing the entire dashboard. There were no more police cars in sight.

"Got 'em!" Supreme bragged.

Justice and Chris felt a great deal of relief. They both relaxed in their seats and sighed loudly, glad they had gotten away.

"Whoa, that was close. We have to get rid of this car, and fast."

"When we get back, we'll burn the motherfucker," Justice replied.

They all agreed, then relaxed and enjoyed the ride. Each one had their own thoughts, but all had one goal: killing Ice!

CHAPTER 10

This last few days had been really hectic, causing Supreme and his crew to always be on point wherever they went. He even beefed up on his arsenal using one of Walid's old connects. He wanted to be ready for whatever was coming their way. Supreme never liked cops after watching them gun down their aunt when they were little. To this day he still blamed them for separating him and his brother, so in his mind, they could get it too.

He and Justice were watching Gabby, Dominique, and Kreasha count up all the money so they could go pick up the next shipment. They had all moved in together because Supreme didn't want to be separated from his brother again. Actually, Justice was waiting to find someone with good credit to finalize the deal for the condo next door, so they could have both places. Dom was staying with them until Donte came home.

The only reason Supreme was able to purchase the one they had now was because of Karen, his psychologist. She co-signed for it for him as long as he kept dropping off some sex here and there. That was a small price to pay for the luxurious place they had, but well worth it.

"Is the money ready yet?" Supreme asked, walking into the dining room.

"Yeah, here you go," Gabby said, getting up and passing him the bag. "I have to go see my mom to give her the money for her rent. I will be back in a hour or so."

"Okay!" Justice said, giving her a kiss. "Preme, let's be out, bro."

They all left out to handle their business. Kreasha and Dominique stayed back to relax. Dom was still hurting from hitting her face on the steering wheel as they were getting away.

"I'm going to take a nice hot bath and let my body

soak in the water for awhile," she told Kreasha as she headed upstairs. She ran their bath water and stepped onto the large whirlpool tub, then leaned back to relax.

"Kreasha, where is the soap?"

Kreasha walked in with a fresh bar of soap and passed it to her. She couldn't help but stare at Dom's curvaceous body. She watched lustfully as Dominique ran the soapy towel all over her chocolate body. While she looked, she wondered how she would react if she touched her. Kreasha was bisexual. She loved men, but frequently explored with women also. She wanted to make a move on Dom, but didn't want to blow it.

"Ouch," Dom hollered when the towel touched the sensitive part of her face.

"Here, let me help you."

Kreasha knelt on the side of the tub, then took the towel out of Dom's hand. Dominique tensed up as she felt Kreasha run the warm towel over her breast.

"Relax," Kreasha hissed softly.

Her emerald eyes concentrated on Dom's body. While doing so, she noticed Dom's breathing had sped up. She was trembling at first, but soon began to relax from Kreasha's smooth touch. Gently she ran the towel over her breast, down to her navel, and between her legs. Dom snapped her legs closed on Kreasha's hand. The feel of the towel rubbing between her legs started to arouse her.

"I can't," Dom whispered.

"You need this, just relax," Kreasha replied, easing her legs apart.

Dom started to pant from the sensation. Kreasha dropped the towel into the water and traced her warm fingers up Dom's thigh. Before she knew it, Dom felt Kreasha's fingers slide into her crevice. Her head went back, with her mouth wide open. Kreasha skillfully worked her fingers in and out of Dom. The pain she once felt was nonexistent. Kreasha's touch started to feel so good to her. It felt different from a man's touch, and she enjoyed it. Dom spread her legs wider so Kreasha could do her work.

While Dom was being pacified with Kreasha's two fingers, Kreasha leaned over and slid her tongue into Dom's open mouth. At first she resisted, but Kreasha persisted until she gave in and started to kiss her back, aggressively holding her head tightly.

"Ummmm," Kreasha moaned as she ran her tongue down to Dom's soft breast.

"Yessssss! Bite me," she replied, feeling Kreasha's teeth gently biting at her nipples. Her moans only encouraged Kreasha to continue seducing her.

She ran her tongue down to Dom's throbbing pussy. Dom pushed her pussy out of the water so Kreasha could get a mouthful. She sucked and licked her right into an orgasm. Dom came so thick, it looked like she had lathered herself with Ivory soap. Kreasha was ready for the next step. She helped Dom dry off and led her into the guest bedroom. Once a chick let her get this far, it was pretty much a wrap. She was an expert at the art of seduction.

Dom stretched out naked across the queen-size bed, to await whatever was about to happen next. Kreasha walked out of the room, then returned with a black bag. She opened the bag up and searched through her huge selection of dildos. They ranged from two- to twelve-inch rubber dicks, some strap on, some manual. Kreasha decided to go with the two-inch anal worker and the ten-inch strap on. Dom watched her undress and strap on the huge black dick.

Kreasha was sexy as hell. The rubber dick fit snuggly against her neatly trimmed vagina. Her titties were small and firm, with nice pointy nipples. As she approached, Dom spread her legs wide, ready to take the massive fake dick into her pussy. Kreasha put Dom's legs on her shoulders and entered her.

"Ooooh! Ooooh! Shiiitt," Dom moaned and groaned as she felt Kreasha hit the bottom of her pussy.

Kreasha stroked her slow until Dom loosened up. Then she sped up and gave Dom deep penetrating thrusts.

"Yesss! Yesss!" Dom hollered. "Fuck me harder! Harder!"

Kreasha jammed in and out of Dom, making her cum twice before she pulled out. They lay side by side, breathing each other's sexual fumes, until Dom drifted off to sleep. Kreasha eased out of the bed, then stood over her with a smile on her face, knowing her job was done.

CHAPTER 11

"My fucking man is sitting up in some fucking hospital while them niggas is walking around freely. Somebody tell me why that is?" Ice snapped.

Nobody said anything. They just sat there with blank expressions on their faces. Ice walked around the table slowly, studying their demeanor. He wanted to see which one would have enough courage to admit they had fucked up.

"I know how to get back at them right now," Tank spoke up.

"I'm listening!"

"Let's take everything they have. I know where all their stash spots are and where he lays his head," Tank said. "I just have one request, and that's don't touch Justice. Even though we're not blood brothers, he's still my brother. It's because of that nigga Supreme we are where we are right now."

"Okay, so I want you to handle that. Nobody's off limits except Justice, but if he comes swinging, he's going down also."

"Don't worry, I'll park him myself if I have to."

"Well, if we all agree, let's handle this shit so we can get back to the money. Nobody fucks with us and lives to brag about it. Strap up and be on point," Ice said, ending their meeting. "Yo, Bub, take a walk with me. I need to holla at you about something."

Bub and Ice walked out of the crib to talk, while Tank loaded up his extra clips because he knew he would need them.

"I want you to keep ya man close, and when y'all take care of the situation with Supreme and his crew, make sure he joins them. Anytime a man wants to spare the enemy, he's not trustworthy," Ice said as they leaned against the car.

"I never liked that motherfucker anyway," Bub replied. "He was just a pawn in a game of chess."

"Cool! Now that we're on the same page, take this as a sign of gratitude." Ice passed him a small envelope containing five grand. "That's for you!"

"I'm going to head over and take care of that other thing we talked about."

"Good, let me know when it's done," Ice said.

They both headed their separate ways. Bub had a mission to complete, and he wanted to get it done by the end of the night.

~ ~ ~

Justice decided it would be best for them to always keep a bunch of shooters around the trap houses, just in case Ice came. He was sure Ice and his squad were still looking for that brief chance to retaliate for his man getting hit. Supreme agreed with him because he knew it would be the safest thing to do.

The police chase still had them on edge. If it wasn't for Supreme's driving expertise, they would all be in prison right now. They were sitting in the living room watching television, when a news reporter appeared on the screen:

"Good Evening! I'm Tracy McGee and our crew is live on Germantown and Erie, in Philadelphia, where just a few days ago a heated gun battle took place leaving one man wounded. Thursday night police were called to the scene when shots were fired. Apparently, a man leaving Max's Steaks was walking toward his car, which is still parked on the scene," the reporter announced as the camera flashed back to the scene of the crime.

"Allegedly, as he was about to get in, an unidentified group of gunmen riding in a Pontiac Grand Prix pulled up to him and opened fire, wounding the man. When police arrived, the victim lay there still holding onto his illegal firearm. Ironically, the victim turned out to be Omar Payne. Payne was a fugitive from justice, who had been running from the law for the past two years. He jumped bail on a homicide he was charged with, stemming from an argument he'd had with his friend. He is now listed in stable condition, after being in critical stages when he first arrived. The shooter or shooters still remain at large. This is Tracy McGee, live from what seems to be a robbery gone wrong. Back to our studio," she said.

Supreme pressed the power button. He couldn't believe they still were talking about that shooting. You would have thought Omar had died or something. The only good thing that came out of it was, Omar wouldn't be coming home any time soon. He figured it all worked out for the better, after all. He just wished the nigga would have checked (died) at the hospital.

~ ~ ~

Donte was sitting in his hospital bed eating the McDonald's food Dominique had bought for him because he didn't want to eat nasty hospital food. He was scheduled to go home tomorrow as long as there were no complications with his wounds.

"Baby, can you pass me my phone?" Donte asked.

Dom reached over on the desk and grabbed his cell phone. Donte smacked her on the ass, then squeezed it. She smiled, then started twerking.

"You're not physically ready for this yet, so quit while you're ahead," she replied.

"When I am ready, I'm gonna tear that ass up."

"I'll be waiting," Dom said, then leaned over and gave him a kiss. "I'll be right back. I have to go get my phone charger out the car."

Dominique walked out and headed downstairs to her car. After she left, Donte realized he had to take a piss. Not wanting to call for a nurse, he slowly lifted up and tried to walk to the bathroom. Instead of standing up over the toilet, he sat down.

"I feel like a lil bitch sitting down to piss," he said out loud to himself. As Donte was finishing up, he heard someone come in the room. "That was quick! Don't come in here, 'cause I don't want you to laugh at me."

He didn't get a response. Just when he was about to say something else, the bathroom door opened. Donte couldn't believe who was standing there.

"What's up, homie? What, you thought you were safe up in this motherfucker? Jokes on you now, my nigga."

"Come on, man, please don't do this to me," Donte begged him.

Those cries fell on deaf ears as he received three shots to the chest.

PSSST! PSSST! PSSST!

No one could hear the shots because of the silencer that muffled the sound. Donte's body slumped over on the toilet, with his eyes wide open in fear. Just to make sure he was finished, another round went to his head, leaving a golf-ball-size hole right between the eyes. The intruder then left before anyone came in to check on Donte.

Ten minutes later Dominique came back in the room

and plugged her phone charger into one of the empty outlets. She looked around for Donte, and when she didn't see him, she walked toward the bathroom. As she got closer, she noticed a reddish liquid coming from the other side of the door. Her first instinct was that he fell trying to take a piss, and she rushed in to help him. Dominique opened the door and almost threw up at the sight of Donte lying there dead.

"Noooooo," she screamed at the top of her lungs.

Dom lifted him up into her arms, unfazed by the blood pouring from his body. A nurse ran in, and when she saw the blood and body, she hit the emergency button. Hospital staff flooded the room with the crash cart, hoping to save their patient, but it was way too late. Two nurses helped Dom out of the room trying to get some order from all the chaos. She was an emotional wreck and needed to be sedated. Police arrived and declared the whole floor a crime scene until they figured out what happened. A couple of homicide detectives were able to calm Dominique down before they sedated her. Then they took her back to the station for questioning.

Ice sat in his car talking on the phone. He saw who he was waiting on and unlocked the door to let him in. Once he closed the passenger door, Ice pulled out in traffic. No words were spoken until they were on I-95.

"Any trouble handling your business?" Ice asked.

"Not at all! It's taken care of. The only way that motherfucker will be able to leave is in a casket."

CHAPTER 12

Around two o'clock in the morning, the ringing of the phone woke Kreasha from her sleep. She nudged Supreme to answer it, but he just turned in the opposite direction falling back to sleep. When it started ringing again, this time he answered.

"Hello?"

The caller was screaming over the phone about something. When Supreme was finally able to put together what she said, he jumped out of bed. He ran out of the room to wake up his brother. Shit had really hit the fan now. After filling Justice in on what had happened, they both got dressed, strapped up, and headed out the door.

"Anybody we see that's part of his team, is dead. Even if it's that nigga Tank," Justice said, pissed off. "Once he sided with the enemy, he became an enemy."

"Say no more!"

Supreme and Dom were riding around in a stolen car, trying to find Ice or anyone affiliated with him. They had a bunch of Supreme's goons watching some of Ice's other spots just in case they showed up there. Justice and Chris was in another stolen car, posted outside of Ice's baby mom house.

Time was creeping by slowly. Everyone was extremely tired of sitting around idly. Dom wanted payback for what they had done to her man. They knew Ice had something to do with it. She thought about how they went from robbing niggas to being one of the biggest dope dealers around. Now people were dying, and it felt like karma was coming back to bite them. She wasn't going out like that though. If she died, she was taking a whole lot of motherfuckers with her.

Just when they thought they weren't going to catch up with any of Ice's guys tonight, Supreme spotted a car cruising up the block slowly. He couldn't see who the driver was, so he tapped Dominique to get her attention.

Dom's heart started beating so fast it almost jumped out of her chest. Supreme quickly called Justice to let him know something was about to go down, and told him to hurry up over there.

Anxiety and nervousness filled Supreme's guts like it always did when he was about to murk a nigga. The car slowly passed by, and he could see it was the nigga Bub and some other young bull in the driver's seat. His phone rang! It was Justice letting him know they were only a block away.

"They just passed us. I'm about to jump on them now," Supreme said anxiously over the Bluetooth system.

"Nah, hold up. Let them get a little further up the block," Justice suggested. "How many of them in the car, bro?"

"I only see two of them."

"Good! Fuck it, let's do this."

Supreme pulled out of the parking space right

behind the car, with his headlights off. He crept along slowly, hoping they didn't see him before it went down. Bub's brakes lights came on as he slowed down near his house. When the passenger door opened, Supreme mashed on the gas pedal, increasing his speed drastically.

"I'm ready," Justice confirmed.

Supreme was zipping down the block full speed now. Bub stepped one foot onto the asphalt, and before he could plant the next one, Supreme was there.

CRASH! He rammed into the back of Bub's car. The impact caused the car to move forward about three feet. Bub and the other guy in the car looked around nervously, not knowing what was going on. Bub jumped back into the passenger's seat. Supreme quickly slammed the stolen car in reverse to get some distance between them. He then stepped on the gas and rammed them again. *CRASH!*

Unsuspecting of what was going on, the young bull

stepped on the gas pedal, attempting to get away. He thought the vehicle behind them was the police, until he saw Supreme in the driver seat. Justice raced up the block full speed trying to cut Bub and his driver off. He stopped suddenly right in front of them, but the young bull cut the steering wheel to the right and flew right past both cars.

BOC! BOC! BOC! BOC!

Justice reached out the window with the .357 and fired.

The young bull heard the shots, but he didn't look back, out of fear. He just ducked down and kept his foot on the gas. Supreme was relentless as he stepped on the gas to catch up with Bub and the driver. Justice went the other way trying to box him in so he couldn't escape. As they were approaching the corner, Supreme could see Justice speeding through the intersection. Bub saw it as well but had no plans on stopping.

"You better not stop, nigga," Bub told the kid.

As they neared the intersection, Bub swerved the car to the right purposely. They banged right into Justice's car, ripping the entire bumper off. He made a quick right up Master Street. Justice made an attempt to follow him, but the sagging bumper slowed him down.

Bub and the young bull sped up the block, but Supreme and Dom were on his ass. They were able to catch them easily. Supreme was now alongside them and rammed Bub's car, causing it to go slightly out of control. Supreme hit them again making it go in the opposite direction. Bub and his driver regained control and continued speeding up the street.

Supreme made a U-turn, bouncing onto the sidewalk. Realizing they had to get them now, he drove down the sidewalk with no regard for anyone. It was a good thing no one was out this time of night. They caught up with them quick.

Bub popped out the passenger window, sitting on the ledge. With a gun in each hand, he began firing away rapidly. The shots echoed throughout the neighborhood. The shots missed Supreme's vehicle, giving Bub and his driver a little distance to find an escape. Justice and Chris were now back in the chase bringing up the rear. Finally the young bull found a hole and went for it. By this time they were racing down Parkway at speeds up to ninety mile per hour. He hit the curb, with his left tires gripping the street, while the right tires were on the cement of the sidewalk. They drove down the block like that until they reached the intersection. Supreme and Justice were right behind them.

Supreme didn't want them to get away. He raised Dom's .40 caliber out the window with his left hand, while his right hand gripped the steering wheel. He fired away, resting his arm on the roof of the car. *BOOM! BOOM! BOOM!*

Dom followed suit and reached out her window firing away also. Bub fired back, exchanging shots in retaliation. Justice sped up to get in on the action and help his brother. Bub turned around to see how close Justice was to them. When he saw how close they were, he aimed at their windshield and fired. The speeding of the cars made him aim off by a few feet, hitting nothing.

"Damn it, lose these motherfuckers," Bub shouted at the kid.

"I'm trying, chill out."

The kid was a very good driver. He had been stealing cars since he was ten, and would out drive the best of them. Supreme still trailed behind them closely. Once he was close enough, he crashed into the back of them. This time they didn't get away. Supreme stayed glued to their tail, pushing them along the way. Bub's car lost control as Justice appeared from nowhere and ran smack into them, pushing them further onto the sidewalk.

The driver of Bub's car swerved from side to side at a rapid speed until he regained control. The left tires hopped off the sidewalk as he sped along the edge of the curb. Supreme gained on them again, then rammed the back of the car, sending it out of control again. Bub hung out the window, firing quickly. Suddenly, the kid lost control. The right side of the car slammed into the stop sign, causing a loud thumping noise before Bub's body was thrown from the vehicle. Seconds later, the car crashed head-on into the fire hydrant.

"Holy shit! You see that nigga fly out that window?" Chris asked, wide-eyed.

"Come on, let's go."

Justice slammed on the brakes and jumped out of the vehicle with his gun held high. As he ran toward the car, he fired multiple shots at the windshield, shattering the glass into tiny pieces.

BOC! BOC! BOC!

He made it to the car only to find the kid slumped over the steering wheel. Justice emptied the rest of his bullets in the driver's seat at close range.

Supreme stopped and backed up hoping to catch

Bub before he attempted to get away. As he backed up, he spotted a pile of clothes that looked to be Bub. Supreme and Dominique jumped out of the car aiming their guns at the pile. When they got close to the body, they got the shock of a lifetime. What appeared before their eyes was enough to make them faint. Dom backpedaled away with her eyes stretched open like she had just seen a ghost.

They both jumped back into the car and pulled off in a hurry. Neither of them could muster up the words about what they just saw. As they sped down the block, police sirens could be heard echoing throughout the entire neighborhood and approaching at a fast pace.

CHAPTER 13

The next day when Justice woke up, he turned on the television. He had been watching every newscast trying to find out what they knew. To his surprise, none of the stations had mentioned a word of the incident. He decided to walk to the corner store to purchase a newspaper.

"I'll be right back, baby. Do you need anything from the store?"

"Bring a Dutch, daddy," Gabby said seductively.

Justice left out the house after tucking his gun into his waist. Call it paranoid, but he constantly looked around as he walked down the street. Nobody knew where they lived, but he'd rather be safe than sorry. He picked up the *Philadelphia Daily News* and a couple of Dutches, then headed back to the crib. Once he was back home, he sat at the kitchen table trying to find what he was looking for. Justice located it quickly. On the very front page, clear as day, he found exactly what he was expecting to find. The headlines read, "Death by Decapitation!" When he opened up to the story, it was a short but straight to the point article about it:

> *Early this morning heavy gunfire was reported in the West Philadelphia area. When police arrived on the scene, they found what turned out to be a nightmare. A dead teenager was slumped over the steering wheel, with several gunshot wounds to the head and chest. There was also a decapitated body of an unidentified man on the ground, not too far from the car. Police found over fifty rounds of ammunition in the vicinity.*
>
> *Apparently during a violent gun battle, teenager Tyheem Madison crashed and threw the unidentified man from the vehicle severing his head from his body. Several feet*

away, police found two handguns which had the man's fingerprints on them. The head of the body is still missing.

Details of what really happened are still unclear at the moment. Anyone with any information, please contact one of the following detectives: Detective Lindsey Giddish at (215) 555-0157 or Detective Robert Pino at (215) 555-0158. All tips will be kept confidential.

Reading those words took Justice back to the scene of the crime. He remembered his brother and Dom damn near puking all over the place as they rushed back to the car and sped away. He still couldn't believe what had happened though. Out of all the murders he committed (and there were a lot), he had never seen anything as gruesome as that.

He needed to get everyone together to make sure they were all on the same page and kept their mouths shut. Shit was really about to hit the fan once Ice's girlfriend received her package. He was sure Ice would want to stop hiding then.

~ ~ ~

"Mommy, can I watch cartoons please?" lil Destiny asked.

"After you eat breakfast."

"Okay, is daddy going to eat with us?"

"He will eat when he gets back from dropping your brother off at school. Come sit down and eat so I can put some clothes in the machine," Markita replied, setting the plate of food on the table.

Lil Destiny rushed over to the table as Kita helped her up into the high chair. She started eating her turkey bacon, eggs, and toast while Kita went to answer her doorbell. It was still early in the morning, so she wondered who it could be. When she opened the door, there was no one on the other side. The only thing she saw was a box covered with gift wrapping paper. Kita bent down and picked the box up. It had weight to it, so she thought it was more of his drugs. She hated when he had work delivered to their home.

After setting the package on the table, she headed upstairs to take a quick shower. She and her daughter had an appointment with her hairdresser at ten, and she wanted to be ready to leave when Ice came home.

“Ahhhhh! Mommy,” Destiny screamed.

“Destiny what’s wrong?” she said, running downstairs.

She rushed into the kitchen to find Destiny looking inside the box.

“I told you about messing with shit that don’t belong to you,” she yelled at her daughter.

“But, Mommy,” Destiny tried to say.

“Don’t ‘But, Mommy’ me,” she replied, walking over to the table.

Kita threw up right there on the table when she saw what was inside the box. She grabbed her daughter and ran upstairs to call Ice.

~~~

"Pull up now!" Supreme said as he spotted Ice getting out of his car.

Chris had received a call from one of his jump-offs saying Ice was at a gas station. He told her to follow them until he arrived. They pulled up in front of the school just in time. Supreme realized he was taking a risk moving on Ice this early in the morning, but it was extremely necessary. They probably would never get this chance again.

Ice needed to pay for what he had done to Donte, and Supreme wanted to strike before Ice's crew did. Ice opened the back door to let his son out, which was double-parked behind a string of vehicles. He slammed the door shut, then trotted quickly off the curb. He stood there as the school buses passed him. As soon as the coast was clear, he hurried across the street.

"Cut him off," Supreme suggested. Chris stepped on
~~~

the gas pedal. Suddenly, a small car cut in front of them. The car inched up the block, slowing Chris up drastically.

"Move!" Supreme shouted furiously. "Damn, this motherfucker is gonna get away. Shit!"

By now Ice had managed to make it across the street. He was now walking toward the school, clutching his son's hand tightly. Chris finally made it to the school's entrance. Many people were entering and leaving the building. Supreme rolled the passenger window down, then raised up in his seat, aiming his gun at Ice. Even with the many people that were crowded around the entrance, Supreme felt like he still had a clear shot at Ice.

All of a sudden Ice stopped. He bent down right in front of the little boy, with his back facing the street. He started tying his son's sneakers.

"Make sure you keep your sneaks tied so you don't mess them up," Ice said.

"I'm fly, right Dad?"

"Yeah, you fly lil man. Just make sure you stay fly no matter what okay?" he said, patting his son's head. Kareem Jr. nodded his head in agreement.

"Get that nigga now for Donte," Chris said.

Supreme squinted his eyes, staring down the nose of the gun. He was sure he had a clear shot on him. He slightly tapped the trigger. The little boy lifted his head up, looking in their direction. The look of innocence on the boy's face made Supreme second-guess the whole idea. He leaned back in his seat. The thought of him missing Ice and hitting his son made him change his mind. "I can't do this. Wait until he's not with his son."

Ice stood up without a clue they were back there. Him and his son jogged cheerfully into the building.

"Pull behind his car," Supreme told Chris.

Chris made a quick U-turn and double-parked directly behind Ice's car. They sat there patiently waiting for him to come back out. Minutes passed by before Chris spotted Ice stepping through the corridor.

"Here he comes now," Chris blurted out.

Supreme released the safety lever on his gun, then inhaled deeply while pushing the door open. He jumped out and stood by the door. He stooped down low, with his gun in his hand. From the backdoor window, he could see Ice crossing the street. Supreme's heart was pumping rapidly, and anxiety filled his gut. He couldn't believe how close he was to finally giving Ice what he rightfully deserved. His hands were starting to sweat a little.

Just as Ice came within two feet of his vehicle, Supreme started creeping along the car. Ice was grabbing the door handle just as Supreme reached the back of the car. He anxiously aimed for Ice's head, using the element of surprise.

Ice saw Supreme's reflection in his peripheral, but it was already too late.

BOC! The gun sounded off.

"Aghhh!" Ice screamed out of fear. He stood there motionless with his eyes stretched wide open. He was so nervous he couldn't move a muscle. All he could do was scream. "Aghhh!" he screamed again.

Suddenly he found enough heart to make himself move. He turned around and dashed into flight.

Supreme ran slowly behind him, firing after each step. He blacked out for a few seconds. The only thing on his mind was killing Ice.

BOC! BOC! BOC!

Supreme was so anxious, he was not even aiming. He was just firing recklessly, hoping he hit him. It was no surprise that not one bullet touched Ice. The people in the area began scattering like roaches, picking their kids up and running around attempting to get out of harm's way. The screams and yells of the people snapped Supreme back to reality. He peeked around and was shocked to see all eyes on him.

He really wanted to chase Ice down and finish the

job, but his mind told him to turn around while he still had a chance. He stood there for seconds before turning around and running back to the car.

"Let's roll, Chris," Supreme hollered.

Supreme couldn't believe he had blown another opportunity to body Ice. It was as if he had nine lives or something.

"I had him right there. I don't believe this shit," he told Chris as they drove away from another crime scene.

CHAPTER 14

Dom, Kreasha, and Gabby were sitting out on the patio, talking about what they were going to do today. Since Donte was murdered, Dom had been depressed. They couldn't imagine how she was feeling, but hoped they would be able to cheer her up with a day of entertainment. Kreasha was even hoping she would maybe get a chance for a round two.

"What time are we leaving?" Gabby asked.

"Depends on how long it takes for y'all bitches to get dressed," Kreasha replied, heading inside.

"Come on, girl, let's go get ready."

Dominique followed Gabby inside. It took them an hour to get ready, before they jumped in the Maybach and headed for the mall. Dom had her .357 tucked safely in her purse, in case someone got out of line. She wouldn't hesitate to put a bullet in a motherfucker's head. She was hoping Justice and Supreme found Ice and Tank before she did.

"Let me let Preme know we'll be back later," Kreasha said, dialing his number.

They spent over $20,000 altogether, and still wanted to do more shopping. Dom felt a whole lot better when she spent money. It felt even better knowing it wasn't her money she spent. After grabbing a bite to eat, they headed home. Nobody was there, so they assumed they were back to getting money. They all laughed, talked, and drank Remy until falling asleep on the couch.

~ ~ ~

Meeting in an executive conference room on the sixth floor of the Federal Building on Market Street were some of the most important people in Pennsylvania. The commissioner, director of the ATF, mayor and deputy mayor, as well as several other law enforcement personnel, were all in attendance.

An emergency meeting was called after multiple shootings all over the city. The first to speak was the mayor, and he was pissed.

"Look, we're here tonight for one reason and one reason only, and that's to put these murderers behind bars for the rest of their lives. My city is in an uproar, and I need some answers right now."

Agent Pryor waited patiently for the mayor to finish before he spoke.

"Obviously there's some type of war going on between these two groups. Why, we have a team of agents working on it as we speak."

"These people are clearly on a mission, and in the process, they're tearing up my damn city, and doing it in a goddamn school zone in front of innocent children," the mayor said, banging his fist on the table. He looked at his deputy mayor. "What's your take on this shit storm?"

Deputy mayor Catrena Alston was a lot more experienced in these matters. In fact, she was the most experienced out of all the mayor's advisors. Clearing her throat and readjusting her skirt, she stood up to speak.

"Actually, sir, I'm inclined to think the agent is right. These two crews are beefing over turf and will harm anyone that gets in their way. Even if it's law enforcement."

"So do we have anything worth discussing before we take a look at the carnage these assholes have caused so far?"

"Well, as far as all agencies go, we've pretty much covered all angles. Everyone's face that was caught on the traffic cameras is at every security checkpoint on BOLO alerts, as well as at the FBI agencies. I suggested we send in a couple of agents to help local police in the apprehension of these dangerous criminals," Agent Pryor replied. "We have video from a couple of the school's cameras, so we can have an idea of what were up against."

"Fine, turn the damn thing on. How much worse could it be?" the mayor blurted out.

While the video played, everyone in the room sat quietly, each in their own thoughts. The tension was so thick you could cut it with a knife. If anyone there had been disillusioned about the threat in the streets, they were no longer.

"Lord have mercy, this is worse than we could have imagined," the mayor said. "I want everyone that can assist us, to help with the capture of these lowlifes. I want my streets back safe like they once were."

Listening attentively to not only what he said but also to what everyone else had to say, the director of ATF agreed to provide the mayor with every resource he could to bring them to justice.

"I think my officers are capable of catching a couple of suspects without dragging in a bunch of federal agents," the commissioner intervened.

"Why are we here then?" Agent Pryor said with attitude.

"Whoa! Whoa! Let's not get into a pissing match!" the deputy mayor said. "What we need now more than ever is interdepartmental cooperation. We have a street war that needs to be handled before innocent bystanders get hurt, or even worse, killed."

"You're right, ma'am! We will help any way we can," the director said apologetically.

"Who will be taking the lead, and who will prosecute these assholes?" Agent Pryor asked.

"We'll figure that out later! Just get these assholes off my streets," the mayor replied, sitting with his forehead resting on his hands. This whole fiasco was giving him a monumental headache, and despite having multiple organizations on the case, he thought it would only get worse.

~ ~ ~

Gabby woke up around two o'clock in the morning, to the sound of moaning. She looked over to where Kreasha and Dom were, and they were still sleeping. The moaning continued, and when she looked toward the television, *Fifty Shades Darker* was on the screen. She watched as Christian and Anastasia were having sex. It turned her on so much, her hand found its way into her pants. She started playing with herself until she came in her panties.

The loud panting woke Kreasha up. Her eyes closed halfway when she noticed what her friend was doing.

"Mmmmm," Gabby moaned.

Kreasha watched as Gabby pulled her pants off, then slid her panties to the side. When she saw her insert her fingers into her love tunnel, her own panties began to moisten. By this time Dom's eyes also were open. She smiled at Kreasha, who was now staring at her. Gabby had now placed not one, not two, but three fingers deep inside her pussy.

"Damn, looks like someone is having an episode," Dom playfully stated.

Embarrassed, Gabby stopped and tried to grab her pants. Dominique kicked them toward the other end of the couch and laughed.

"You don't have to be embarrassed, Gab. We all did the same thing every time we watched that movie," Kreasha said. "I have an idea!"

Kreasha stood up and allowed her dress to drop to

the floor. Standing there naked, she walked over to where Gabby was sitting, and grabbed her hand. Gabby looked in Dom's direction.

"I tried it before, and it was great," she whispered.

Kreasha led her upstairs to her room, with Dom right behind them. Once in the room, Kreasha went over and lay on the bed. Gabby followed suit and climbed into the bed as well. Kreasha leaned over and kissed her. Their tongues probed as they explored one another intimately. She laid Gabby back and parted her thighs to reveal her pinkness. Kreasha dove in face-first, getting a mouth full.

She started to flick her tongue quickly across Gabby's clitoris. Gabby responded by gyrating her body into Kreasha's face. Kreasha's tongue darted in, out, and all around Gabby's pussy in a way she was very familiar with. She suddenly became aware Dom was positioning herself over her face. Without hesitance, she flicked her tongue out sampling Dom's sweetness.

"Oh wow, that tastes so good," Kreasha mumbled.

Gabby's pussy ran like a faucet for what seemed like minutes. She was susceptible to their every whim, and she hated for it to end. She was still horny as they switched positions.

"Let's see what you can do?" Dom requested.

At this point, Gabby couldn't do anything but oblige. She too had a tongue game that was way too official, and now it was her turn to show them how she got down. From that moment, they all formed a bond. Whenever the men were away, they would play. It wasn't like they were cheating with other men. They were three women, keeping each other happy, and happy they were, when it was all said and done.

CHAPTER 15

"Bro, we need to get home so we can count this money," Supreme stated.

"You go ahead, and I'll meet you there. I'm about to handle something real quick," Justice yelled out. Supreme already knew what was going on when he saw him pulling some bad-ass chick out back with him.

"Alright, but hurry up and get your ass home."

"Yes, Pop!" Justice sarcastically replied.

Supreme carried the two duffle bags out to his car and put them in the trunk. Before getting into the driver's seat, he turned and looked at the trap house. He had a feeling he shouldn't leave his brother there by himself, especially with all the shit going on. He shook his head and brushed it off as paranoia. Supreme headed home so he could get the women to do what they loved, and that was count money.

"Hold on for a minute," the chick said.

She slipped her shoes on and followed him out back away from the house. They walked in the cut where they could be away from everybody. He stared at her body and wondered what she looked like without those pants.

"Take them clothes off."

For several seconds she stood there reluctant to comply. After looking at his face and seeing how handsome he was, she knew she was giving him whatever he wanted. Slowly she slid her pants off, followed by her shirt. Knowing he had her, he removed his jeans.

"Now what?" she asked seductively.

"Get on your knees and suck my dick like your life depends on it."

Without further hesitation, she dropped to her knees, wrapped her hand around his limp dick, and proceeded to rapidly lick her tongue around the mushroom tip. She took his gradually growing piece of meat into her mouth, and stroked his nut sack with her left hand.

Justice leaned his head back and looked at the sky.

"Oh, shit, bitch! That's right, suck this dick. You keep sucking like this, I'ma get hooked," he moaned.

She continued to blow his mind with the bomb-ass blow job she was giving him. Justice was in a zone.

"Like that, daddy?" she whispered.

"Yes! If your pussy is anything like your head game, I'm whipped."

The girl paid no mind to what he said. She'd heard it all before, plenty of times. She was so into it, she didn't realize he was ready to bust, until he grabbed her head, forcing his dick down her throat. Fortunately, her gag reflexes were superb. All ten inches slid down her throat as he released his load. He slid back out of her mouth, leaving her panting aggressively.

"You already know I gotta take a look at that pussy. Baby, lay down and spread them legs," he said, looking down at her. He was still rock hard.

The girl rolled over and gathered her clothes

together to lie on. She settled onto the ground and opened her legs, revealing her pretty pink pussy. Justice smiled, anticipating having his way with her. He'd waited long enough and was ready to stick his dick in her young, beautiful pussy. It looked like it was wet and tight.

Justice watched her as he stroked his dick with his hand, making sure it was fully erect. Then he smiled even more to see her stroking her pussy, getting it ready for him. She licked her lips and moaned, enticing him further. Justice obliged and sunk to the ground between her legs. With lightning-fast speed, he rammed his dick into her hot box, causing her to squirm from the pressure and pain.

"Ohhhhhhh, wow!" she screamed, and raked her nails along his back.

He slid his dick out and back against the walls of her dripping wet pussy. She panted, hugging his dick inside her. It was so tight, just as he imagined. Her other sexual encounters were nothing like what she was feeling at this moment. Justice took a deep breath and tried to move back to long strokes again. He couldn't get enough of her and wanted more. Without warning, she came, her tight pussy squirting cum all over his hard dick.

"I'm cummmming," she continued to scream as nut dripped out of her pussy and onto her clothes.

"Damn, bitch, you got that fire!" He pulled out and looked at his cum-coated dick, then watched as her body trembled and shook like crazy. "Fuck this!"

He entered her again, his huge dick parting her pussy lips like the Red Sea. Sliding in and out, he looked at her beautiful face. Her eyes were doing acrobats in their sockets. Justice slid his hand behind her head and held it up to his chest while never missing a stroke. In and out he went, thinking to himself this was one of the best pussies he had ever had.

Stroking deep into her pussy, he aggressively started

fucking her wildly. He let go of her head and lifted her legs onto his shoulders, licking the sole of her left foot. He ran his tongue down the soft flesh of her foot. She wiggled her toes, and he stuck the big one into his mouth, sucking it. She wished he would have taken her to a hotel instead of the backyard.

"Oh shiiittt," she moaned, biting her bottom lip.

Just put all his weight into his strokes as his dick pounded her pussy. Hitting something deep inside her, he eased up just a bit, then slammed back into her moistness. She squirmed and panted underneath him.

"Turn over, baby," he instructed, twisting her legs off his shoulders.

As she turned, her legs continued to shake uncontrollably. Justice grabbed ahold of her waist in an attempt to hold her steady. She tried to do as he asked, but was out of breath and shaking from multiple orgasms. She prepared herself to be fucked doggy style. She'd only been in that position a few times, and loved it. Her pussy continued to jump as he ran his hand over and around her swollen folds, smearing the juices that flowed freely between her legs. A feeling of uneasiness came over her when his thumb caressed the hole of her rectum. He rubbed it in circular motions, until, without warning, he shoved it in her ass as far as he could.

"Ouuchh," she screamed, falling flat on her stomach trying to escape the painful pressure.

"Get back in position," Justice said, his voice sounding demon-like. "From this point on, you're my bitch, and you might as well get used to being fucked like this, understand?"

"Okay, do what you like," she said, whimpering, but still willing to please him.

Justice chuckled to himself. As if he needed her permission! Grabbing his dick, he gently placed the tip into her ass. He moved slowly, allowing her muscles to contract and get used to it. He knew it was her first time, and that further excited him. He kind of felt sorry for not taking her to a motel, or even to a bed, for that matter.

“Ohhhh damn,” he moaned out as his dick slid further into her tight hole.

The girl screamed as if she was being murdered, and as he pushed in to her a second time. He was glad they were outside where no one could hear them.

“Whewwwwww,” she screamed again, loud enough to wake the neighbors if there were any around. Her cries excited him even more. He had gotten into a rhythm, running his dick in and out of her asshole.

“Take this dick like a good bitch. You love this dick, don’t you?” he grunted, continuing to long stroke her ass.

She lay flat on her stomach, no longer able to withstand the cruel punishment he was putting down on her backside. The pain was so excruciating, she had to struggle to stay conscious.

“You better not ever let no one fuck you like this. You hear me?” He felt his load building its way up to the tip of his dick.

"Yessssss!" she yelled. "Yessssss, baby!"

"Flip over," he said, pulling his dick out.

She turned over just in time to feel his hot nut squirt all over her face. He stood over her stroking his dick, making sure he released the entire load. Justice fixed his clothes while the girl hurriedly grabbed her own clothes and proceeded to get dressed.

"When will I see you again?" she asked.

"When you tell me where I can find your brother so I can give him what I owe him," Justice replied, rubbing her ass gently.

Talia was Ice's younger sister. Justice had found out through a mutual friend that she was trying to get at him. She was unaware of the beef between the two, so when Justice saw her outside the trap house with her friends, he invited her in. She was so into him, she willingly gave up her brother's whereabouts, along with her body. Justice had a smile on his face as he drove down the street. He knew exactly where to find Ice. He had been under his nose the whole fucking time.

~ ~ ~

Ice was sitting in the cut on a stoop across the street from all the action that was going on. Ever since Justice had stopped coming around, his block was once again popping. He wasn't paying the slightest attention to the traffic flow, because he was busy talking to his girl on the phone.

"Let me get two," the raggedy-looking fiend demanded as he stood there impatiently.

"Give me one," another man screamed as he approached the boy. Together they boxed him in. The kid looked down, separating the packets so he could serve them.

"Nobody move!" the raggedy fiend aimed his gun at the boy's chest as he grabbed him by the collar.

The first fiend drew his gun as well, aiming it at the small crowd that was huddled up at the alleyway, waiting to get served.

"Empty your pockets, and I want you to take me to the stash," the dope fiend said nervously.

Ice looked up and noticed the robbery in progress. He did a double take to make sure his eyes weren't playing tricks on him. He ended the call, without saying bye to his girl. He quickly got up from the stoop and ran off of the curb. He reached underneath his shirt for his 9mm. He was so anxious to get over to the robbery, he didn't even see the filthy-looking dope fiend who was crossing his path.

BOOM!

The dope fiend fired, hitting Ice in the gut, at close range. As he tumbled backward, the fiend fired another shot from the rusty .357.

BOOM!

Ice collapsed on the ground, landing in a seated position. Just as he hit the ground, his finger pressed the trigger of his own gun, hitting nothing.

BOC! BOC! BOC!

The man ran away from Ice, meeting the two other fiends in the middle of the street. The one that was holding the kid by the collar looked at the one who shot Ice.

"Go finish him now!" he demanded.

"The cops are coming," the guy replied.

"Man, fuck it, I'll do it myself," the fiend stated.

The other two ran to the getaway car parked near the corner. He started to head over where Ice was lying, then spun back around quickly. The fiend walked back toward the other two before they could pull off. They saw him coming and waited, thinking he was rolling with them.

BOCA! BOCA! BOCA! BOCA!

He put two bullets in each of their heads, not wanting to leave any ties back to him. After doing that, he ran toward Ice hoping to finish the job, but there were a bunch of people surrounding him. He wasn't crazy enough to run into a crowd of people. Besides, Ice wasn't moving, so he assumed he had checked (died) already. He ran back to his car and made a clean getaway.

A couple blocks away, Justice pulled his car over to change his clothes and wipe the dirt off his face. It was him who set the whole thing up with Ice. He was just hoping the two real fiends he had hired handled their business before meeting their own demise. He had to rush, because he could hear the sirens in the distance, approaching really fast.

As soon as he pulled back out in traffic, out of nowhere, two unmarked cars sped head-on, cutting him off. Justice put the gear in reverse, trying to escape. He peeked in his rearview mirror, and two more cars were boxing him in from the rear, leaving him with nowhere to run.

To his right, a black work truck was already blocking him off. It pulled close to his door, trapping him inside his vehicle. Once he saw all the badges flashing, he raised his hands high in the air, making sure the police saw them.

"Damn!" he shouted, thinking of the gun hiding under his passenger seat and the hot one locked in the glove compartment.

Police officers jumped from every vehicle with their guns aimed at him. What scared him the most was the fact that he had just smoked two motherfuckers with one of the guns. He hoped they didn't find it. If they did, he wouldn't ever see the streets again.

"Police, don't fucking move!" they shouted aggressively.

"What the fuck?" Justice asked as they dragged him violently out of the car, handcuffed him, then threw him in the backseat of a marked car.

"We got your ass now," one of the men in all black smiled. "Get him out of here!"

Justice could see everyone giving each other high

fives and shaking hands like it was the biggest bust ever. He wondered what all they had on him. He would soon be finding out, and that would determine his fate.

CHAPTER 16

Supreme was asleep when he received the phone call about his brother getting knocked. He immediately contacted one of the best criminal lawyers in the country to represent him. Supreme was supposed to meet up with him today, but every time he called, his secretary said he was in court on another case. Just when he was about to say fuck him, he received a call.

"What's up?"

"I apologize for the holdup. I've been looking over your brother's case and it's not looking good at all. The two guns they found carry six to ten years alone, and then he has an even bigger problem. The attempted murder of that kid. He could be looking at another ten to fifteen years, or worse if the kid's family decides to pull the plug. Oh, and the alphabet boys are the ones holding him. It was some kind of joint operation."

"Fuck, man, we have to get my brother out of this

situation. When you wanna meet?" Supreme asked.

"Uh, I'm free right now. How about you?"

"I ain't doing nothing. Where do you want me to meet you at?"

"It doesn't matter to me. I'm in my car now. Where you at?"

"I'm on the block! I mean, I'm on Lindenwood Street," Preme told him.

"Alright, I'll meet you right there. I'll hit you when I get close."

Supreme disconnected the call wondering what kind of lawyer meets people on the block. As he was sitting there, he hoped those feds didn't try no crazy shit. He was going to do whatever it took to get his brother out. The ringing of his phone interrupted his sentimental moment.

"Yo, what's up?"

"Where you at, kid? I'm here!"

Supreme looked around in search of the lawyer. An

all-black Aston Martin came cruising up the block. The sun was bouncing off the chrome rims, blinding everyone on the block. The beauty of it had Supreme captivated.

"What the fuck is that? This you in the black car?"

"Yeah! It's me, my friend," he replied.

"Here I go right here," Supreme said, flashing his high beams.

The deep tinted vehicle double-parked right next to Supreme. He finally realized it was Larry Savino driving the Aston Martin DB9 convertible. Supreme jumped out of his vehicle and stood next to the beauty. Larry cracked the tinted window.

"Get in kid," he shouted.

"Cool!"

Supreme peeked around sneakily. He felt more like he was about to make a drug deal than meet with an attorney. He hopped in and shut the door. The sounds of Jay Z and Kanye West ripped through the speakers.

Haziness filled the car as Larry blew a cloud of cigar smoke from his mouth.

"What's up? It's a pleasure to finally meet you," Larry said, with the cigar dangling from his mouth.

They shook hands before Larry pulled off slowly. Supreme couldn't believe what he was seeing. The lawyer that came highly recommended by so many people was sitting in the driver seat, leaning real low like a pimp. The reflection from his huge sparkling earrings bounced crazily all over the black leather interior, like a disco light.

"So what it look like?" Supreme asked.

"A case like this will start off at twenty grand easily. That's if we can avoid a trial, which is unlikely," he said, looking at Supreme to see how he reacted to the numbers.

Supreme's facial expression stayed the same, due to the fact that money wasn't an option when it came to his brother. "No problem!"

"Alright, but I tell you this. I want to try something first, if it's okay with you? I'm not trying to kill you with the price, so if I can save you some money, I'll feel a whole lot better."

"I'm listening," Supreme said, giving him his undivided attention.

"First and foremost, in order for this to work, I'm going to schedule an evidentiary hearing to try and win this at the preliminary. If it don't work, we will definitely be taking this to trial."

"No doubt! So what will you have to do differently?" Supreme wondered.

"As his attorney, I'm gonna suggest he stays far away from the business until this is all over and we find out what all the feds have. Off the record though, if someone was to make sure the witnesses never talks, that would be great. A little pressure may do the trick."

"I like the way you think," Supreme told him.

"But before that happens, I want to try something

risky. That is where you come into play, my friend. Here's what I want you to do . . ."

~ ~ ~

Tank was walking around nervous as hell. He never thought about what he was getting into by turning against his family. He had let pussy come between his brothers and now his money. None of his team was making any money right now because of Ice being on a life support machine. Now he was ready to go back to what he knew best.

"Y'all trying to do this or what?" Tank asked. He was sitting in the car with two lil niggas that had been working for Ice. They were ruthless young bulls that would do anything for a dollar. Both of them nodded their heads in agreement. "Let's go!"

Walking through her house in a red lace Victoria's Secret bra and panty set, Yetta reached the closet. She put her cleaning supplies away, and closed the door. She followed her daily routine of cleaning her house in her underclothes while listening to Beyoncé. She headed to the bathroom to take a shower. She had to pick up her nephews from daycare because her sister had to work late.

Stepping inside the steamy shower, Yetta allowed the water to cascade down her voluptuous body. She had a little over an hour before she had to grab the boys, so she decided to spend a little extra time in the shower. The hot water was soothing as she closed her eyes and relaxed in its comfort. Just then she heard the shower curtain being snatched down from its rods. Before she could open her eyes, she felt a sharp pain shoot across her cheekbone.

"Nooooo," she screamed in pain. Another punch shut her right up when she felt her nose break.

Blood rushed down her face with the shower water as she fell, shocked and stunned, to the floor of the porcelain tub. Before Yetta could regain her senses, she felt her body being carried, half dragged, out of the bathtub, across the floor and into her bedroom. She tried kicking violently and screaming at the top of her lungs.

She hoped her neighbor heard her and came to help. She then felt the weight of a man as he dropped down on her chest with his knees. Yetta choked in an attempt to regain her breath. It felt like he had cracked her sternum. She lay defenseless on her bedroom floor as they duct taped her hands together. Her eyelids had swollen up the size of golf balls, but she was able to see there were two men that had attacked her. She was sure they were on some rape shit, until the one who sat on her chest spoke up.

"Save me the trouble of violating you in the worst way possible, okay? You can make it easy if you tell me where the dope and money is, and don't you try to play on my intelligence. I know who you're holding for, and I want it all," Tank ordered.

Lying there in total shock, Yetta almost wished they were there to rape her. At least then she wouldn't be faced with having to commit the unthinkable sin of betraying her brother. Yetta was the sister of one of a ruthless drug cartel. They were connected with the same group of people that supplied Supreme and Justice. She was there to drop off over ten kilos of heroin for her brother.

Tank had ridden with Supreme before, so he knew this was around the time of the week she would make her drops. She always used her nephews' daycare as the meet spot, so she didn't mind picking them up. There was no way Yetta was telling them anything about the stash.

"Okay, this bitch must think it's a game. Turn her over on her stomach, and go get me a broom," he stated.

"What?" one of the dudes said, surprised.

"We're going to see how far it will go up her ass before she decides to open her fucking mouth."

"Okay, okay, please! I already got rid of everything. You're an hour too late, I swear."

As if he hadn't heard a thing she said, the taller of the two left the room. He came back moments later with a cynical smile plastered across his face. He handed the broom to Tank, then grabbed Yetta's ankles and rolled her over. Yetta could only moan with fear and pain. Tank gripped the broom tightly while looking down at her ass. Finally, he made up his mind and tossed the broom aside.

"We don't need no damn stick to punish this bitch," he told his two partners.

He pulled down his pants, and Yetta could see his monstrous dick. It was every bit of twelve inches long, and as fat as a bottle. She could only imagine the excruciating pain his penis would inflict on her virgin ass. She relented and nearly screamed.

"I'll tell you! Okay, I'll tell you everything you want to know."

"I just bet you will, bitch, but you should've told me before you awoke the sleeping giant," he said, referring to his dick. "Now you get to put him back to sleep."

The next thing she knew, Tank was positioning himself on top of her. She was scared to death and hoped it would be over quick.

"What type time you niggas on?" said a familiar voice.

Tank turned around, and standing by the door with a MAC-10 pointed at them was Chris. He was staying next door so he could finish the deal with Yetta and maybe fuck her again like they had the last time he copped. He heard her scream and knew something was wrong. Any other time he wouldn't have been playing Captain Save-a-Hoe, but this was about money, and no one gets in the way of that. What surprised him was who was trying to assault her. He had finally caught his traitor-ass adoptive brother with his pants down, literally. Tank's facial expression said just that.

"Chris!" he said, surprised.

One of the men tried to draw on him, but was caught

by a bullet to the side. The pain was blunt and brutal but only lasted for a few seconds because the next two bullets hit him in the face. One under his right eye, and the other in his forehead. Blood, brain, and bone fragments splattered out the back of his skull, onto his partner's clothes. The other guy tried to get out of sight, but was also rocked to sleep with three precise shots to the chest.

Through all the commotion, Tank tried to scramble off of Yetta and pull his pants up. Seeing his friends slaughtered in cold blood and the MAC-10's aim shifting toward him, Tank threw his hands in the air.

"Hold on, bro. Let's talk about this!" he said.

"Shut the fuck up, and lay your bitch ass on the floor."

Before Tank could move, Yetta kicked him in the nuts, causing him to bend over in pain, then kneed him in the face. She looked at Chris with grateful relief.

"Keep his bitch ass right there, okay?" she said.

Yetta walked into the other room to grab her cell phone out of her purse. She locked the front door and made her way back to the bathroom, where Chris had Tank held hostage. When she turned around and saw her reflection in the mirror, she was crushed. Her face was swollen and covered in dried up blood.

Turning on the water in the sink, she cupped her trembling hands and splashed handfuls of cold water on her face. She hoped she would open her eyes and find it was all a dream. This was anything but a dream though. This was as real as it gets; her face was a testament to that. She turned the water off, grabbed a towel off the rack, then carefully wiped her swollen face dry. Next, she called her brother.

He answered on the third ring, and she didn't even give him a chance to say anything other than, "Hey!" before blurting out everything that had transpired, from almost being raped, to the demise of two of the assailants.

"Take the phone to the bull," her brother said through clenched teeth.

Yetta did as she was told, knowing he was beyond mad. When she went back into the bedroom, Chris was standing over the bodies, with his gun still aimed at Tank. She walked over and passed Chris the phone.

"Here, my brother on the phone. He wants to talk to you."

Chris took the phone without a second thought and was going to speak, when Tank blurted out something from where he was lying on the floor.

"Come on, man, I'll do anything. Just please don't kill me."

Yetta grabbed the glass vase sitting on her nightstand and smashed it over Tank's face. His face was covered in blood. She looked at Chris and gave him a head nod, letting him know to answer her brother.

"What's up, Ray?"

"I have a cleanup crew on their way to you right

now. They should be there within the hour. If you could just make sure that motherfucker doesn't ever breath again, I would appreciate it. The new order is on me, so let your brothers know we're all good. I'm sure they will be very happy with that."

"Good looking," Chris said excitedly. "Don't worry about that nigga; he dug his own grave the day he went against us."

"Once again, I'm very grateful for what you did. You and your brothers now have the keys to the city. Enjoy, my friend, and give my blessings to Justice. Let him know if he needs me to do anything, I'm just a phone call away," Ray said, then ended the call before Chris responded.

Chris wondered how the hell Ray knew Justice was booked. He looked at Yetta, then looked down at Tank, who was starting to recover from the blow to his face. He pointed the MAC-10 at his head.

"Chris, come on, bro. We were brothers before that

nigga came on the scene. Who snuck you food when Mom Mom locked us in that room, huh?" Tank questioned, trying to turn Chris against his team.

"Too late for that, bro. See you in hell!"

BOC! BOC! BOC! BOC! BOC! BOC!

CHAPTER 17

"Smith, you have a visit," the correctional officer yelled over the loudspeaker, then clicked Justice's cell door.

Justice got up and brushed his teeth again, then threw on his crisp uniform he had folded under his mattress. Once he was ready, he exited his cell and walked to the front to be buzzed off the block. After getting searched, Justice walked into the visitation area, where Gabby awaited. He gave her a passionate kiss and a hug before sitting down to converse.

"How are you hanging in here, baby?" Gabby asked emotionally.

"I'm good! I just want to get the fuck out of here. Why hasn't anyone posted my bail yet?"

"Baby, your bail is almost two million dollars. They did that shit on purpose so you couldn't get out, and if we were to pay it, the feds would want to know how.

However, I do have some good news." Justice looked at her, waiting for her to continue with the news. "Your adoptive brother is now swimming with the sharks, thanks to Chris."

"Chris?" Justice said, surprised.

"Yeah, Chris was at the spot grabbing the re-up, and bull was trying to pull a lick against the wrong people. Also, Preme told me to tell you the other issue is a dead end, and you shouldn't worry."

"Say no more," Justice said, cutting her off, knowing how the feds get down. They could be recording their conversation right now. "Why didn't Preme come?"

"He sends his love and said he will see you when you get home. He also told me to tell you to dress to impress when you come to court, because there's gonna be a circus," she said, referring to the media.

"I'll be ready. Don't worry!" he replied, giving Gabby another kiss. "So you wanna take a walk to the ladies' room?"

"What about them?" she asked, pointing to the two guards at the desk.

"They're cool, baby! I told you they're on my payroll. Now come on, because we only have twenty minutes left."

Justice gave the CO a head nod as they slid into the ladies' room and locked the door. No time for foreplay, Gabby pulled her dress up, revealing she wasn't wearing any panties, then bent over on the sink.

"Fuck me hard, papi," Gabby moaned as Justice entered her from behind.

Justice gave her exactly what she wanted, trying to rip her pussy to shreds. He only lasted five minutes due to the fact that he hadn't had sex in a while. He erupted deep inside Gabby, then pulled out slowly making sure all of his seed stayed in. Gabby was a bit frustrated he came so early and she didn't reach her own orgasm. She knew they only had limited time, so she was happy she was able to please her man. She would get hers later when they had ladies' night. She smiled to herself just thinking about their last rendezvous.

"I will see you tomorrow in court," Gabby said as they exited the bathroom.

Justice gave her another kiss, then headed back to his cell. He sat on his bunk, wondering how this was all going to play out. He was charged with murder along with a list of other charges and would never be coming home if found guilty. He hoped his lawyer was as good as he said he was. Larry had told him he had a trick up his sleeve, and Justice hoped he used it before the grand finale.

~ ~ ~

Justice sat in the crowded courtroom, wearing his federal-issued inmate uniform. Larry thought it would be a good idea for everyone to see him looking like a citizen that was guilty until proven innocent. He glanced around the courtroom. To his right were a bunch of federal agents looking very confident this would be an open-and-shut case. Behind them were two women, and a man he thought he had seen on TV before. The agents waved at him in a teasing manner. Justice, in return, stuck his middle finger up at them before turning away. They wouldn't miss this hearing for the world.

Aggravation was setting in on the faces of Judge McGee and the prosecutor. Justice looked at the clock and started getting nervous. His lawyer still hadn't arrived yet. Through all the other court dates, Larry had never shown up late. He was normally there before anyone else. His brother hadn't come to any of his court dates either. Justice was wondering what was going on.

"Where the fuck is he at?" he mouthed to Gabby, who was sitting a few rows behind him. Chris and Kreasha were also there supporting their family.

She shrugged her shoulders, looking confused. She was about to leave she could try to call him, when Dominique walked in. She whispered something in

Gabby's ear, who then looked over at Justice with a thumbs up.

"Mr. Smith," the judge shouted. "Your attorney better have a good reason to be holding me up, or else," he said in a threatening manner.

Everyone focused their attention on Justice to see his reaction. They were expecting a smart remark to come out of his mouth. He was known for making slick comments in court, but today he had something differently planned for them. He kept his mouth shut and didn't even respond, kind of shocking the crowd of onlookers.

The mahogany double doors suddenly flew open unexpectedly. The noise caught everyone's attention, causing them to turn in their seats as Larry made his grand entrance. He stepped down the aisle with his head held high, holding his briefcase. He made it to the area where Justice was sitting, and placed his hand on his shoulder.

"Sorry, man," he whispered. "I had to make sure some last-minute plans were ready to go."

He looked over to the prosecutor, who was frowning his face at him. Larry quickly turned to the judge's bench. The judge was also furious with Larry's tardiness.

"Uh, Mr, Savino, do you have anything you would like to say?" Judge McGee asked.

"I apologize for being late. Something came up on the way here."

"It must have been really important; you showed up in my courtroom an hour late," the judge said sarcastically. "Are you ready to start these court proceedings?"

"Yes, I'm ready, your honor," Larry replied, opening his briefcase.

"Well, please take that smirk off your face like you run this courtroom. This is my domain, and you will respect it, understand?"

"Yes, your honor, I do!"

The prosecutor chuckled quietly as he watched the big-time lawyer get put in his place. Larry looked the prosecutor square in the eyes and winked at him devilishly. This enraged him even more.

"Let's begin!" the judge demanded.

"The United State versus Smith," a voice screamed from afar.

The prosecutor cleared his throat as he looked through his stacks of papers sitting before him on the table. Justice slouched back in his seat.

"Your honor, on January 12, 2017, Rajon Henderson, also known as Bub, along with a juvenile name James Rollins, was murdered execution-style on a city street. I have several witnesses that are willing to take the stand and identify that man, Justice Smith, who also is a juvenile, as the murderer," he said, pointing to Justice.

Justice stared coldly into the prosecutor's eyes,

showing no intimidation. Larry sat there wiping dust from his glasses. His cockiness was evident to everyone in the room.

"Mr. Savino, do you have any argument?" the judge asked.

"No, I just want to start the proceedings," Larry said arrogantly. "Bring the witnesses on."

"Okay," the prosecutor said sarcastically. "That I will do! I'd like to call my first witness, Ms. Ellen Brown, to the stand."

The raggedy-looking woman walked slowly to the stand. They swore her in before she took her seat.

"Ms. Brown, where were you on the afternoon of January 12, 2017?" the prosecutor asked.

"I was standing on the corner talking to my friend," she whispered softly.

"Can you explain to the courtroom what you saw on that day?"

"I was walking down the block when I heard loud

gunshots. I immediately started running, and the next thing I know, I was laying flat on my face."

"Ms. Brown, why were you laying on your face?" he asked.

"I got shot in my calf."

"Oh, I see," he said sarcastically. "Ms. Brown, please tell the courtroom what your purpose was for being on that block at that particular time?"

"I was purchasing heroin," she whispered shamefully. "At that time, I was an addict."

"Ms. Brown, would the brand of heroin you were purchasing happen to be the famous Lucifer?"

"Your honor, what is the relevance of that question?" Larry said, standing up.

"That's enough of that," the judge said strictly.

"I apologize, your honor," the prosecutor said. "Ms. Brown, do you see the man who shot you in the courtroom?"

"Yes, I do," she replied, hanging her head low.

"Where is he, ma'am? Can you please point him out for the court?"

The woman pointed directly to Justice, who just shook his head with fury. She turned away after she pointed him out.

"Let the record show that she pointed to the defendant, Justice Smith," the prosecutor said. "No further questions for this witness."

"Thank you, Ms. Brown," the judge said. "Mr. Savino, would you like to cross-examine the witness?"

"No, your honor," he said quickly, without even lifting his head. He just examined his newly manicured fingernails.

Justice looked at him with an agitated look on his face. He nudged Larry with his elbow, but he ignored him. Justice hoped Larry didn't blow the trial for him in an attempt to prove something to the prosecutor.

"Okay, I would like to call my next witness to the stand," the prosecutor said.

And older man took the stand next, and after being sworn in, Justice listened to him make accusations as well. Afterward, the judge gave Larry the chance to cross-examine, but once again he refused. Justice was now furious with Larry's lack of effort.

The prosecutor called two more witnesses, and they both agreed Justice was the shooter who shot them and the two deceased. Larry didn't cross either of them. The prosecutor called to the stand his fifth witness.

"I'd like to call Mr. Jihad Walker to the stand."

Of all the names, this one rang a bell in Justice's head. He sat up attentively, wondering where he had heard that name before. Who he saw before his eyes almost shocked him to death. Ice was at the witness stand, getting sworn in. He had on corrections clothes also.

"Mr. Walker, where were you on the day of January 12, 2017?" the prosecutor asked.

"Dropping my son off at school."

"Explain to the courtroom what happened that day," the prosecutor suggested.

"I was coming out of the building, when I heard gunshots ringing off," he said clearly.

Justice couldn't believe his ears or his eyes. He was shocked the infamous Ice had turned into a snitch.

"Bitch-ass nigga," he said to himself.

"Mr. Walker, tell the court how many times were you shot."

"Once in my stomach."

"Excuse me, Mr. Walker, did you say your stomach?"

"Yes!" Ice mumbled.

"I thought you said 'attempted murder,'" the prosecutor said sarcastically. "Mr. Walker, do you see the man in this courtroom who shot you?"

The prosecutor looked at Larry smiling from ear to ear as if he'd proven a point. Justice still couldn't believe this was happening. Neither could Chris and

Dominique, who were sitting there with their mouths wide open.

"No, I don't," Ice said loud and clear without hesitation, causing everyone to gasp for air.

"Mr. Walker, perhaps you didn't hear my question correctly. I said, do you see the shooter in this courtroom?"

"Like I said before, no, sir, I don't," he repeated.

"Mr. Walker, are you telling me the man sitting to my left is not the shooter?" the prosecutor blurted out, showing signs of anger.

"Your honor," Larry said, furious.

"Overruled," the judge said. "Proceed!"

"I never saw that man a day in my life," Ice lied.

Listening to this, Justice was totally confused. He wondered why Ice suddenly had a change of heart.

"I've been in Fort Dix trying to get my shit together," Ice began. "The prosecutor's office has been visiting me twice a week since I've been down. I told them I didn't know who shot me, but they insist on making me know."

Larry smirked at the prosecutor. The room was so quiet at the change of events. No one had seen this coming.

"Your honor, it's obvious some sort of foul play is involved in the matter," the prosecutor claimed. "Nevertheless, I have one more witness I would like to call to the stand, if I may?"

"Your honor," Larry interrupted. "I've sat quietly for forty minutes, to be exact, while Mr. Lugo has called witness after witness to the stand. Whatever point he has to prove, I guess he's proven it," he said. "I have only one piece of evidence to show, and of course the decision is yours after that. May I present it?" Larry asked, opening his briefcase.

"Proceed," the judge demanded.

Justice and the rest of the courtroom wondered what this piece of evidence could be. Larry carried the evidence in a leather carrying case. He slammed the case onto the judge's desk.

"Here it is, your honor, plain and simple."

"Open it!" the judge insisted.

The whole room was quiet at this point. They were all anxiously waiting to see what he was hiding inside the case. Larry unzipped the case and pulled a small flash drive from it.

"Play this please," he asked the bailiff.

The bailiff grabbed the flash drive and made his way over to the monitor. He plugged the flash drive in and located the file as Larry instructed.

"Your honor, I've recorded all the witnesses' statements," Larry said. "Each of them stated they were shot around the same area and time. They all agreed, correct me if I'm wrong, your honor."

"Go ahead!"

The video began to play for the courtroom. The Cheesecake Factory in the Christiana Mall appeared on the screen.

"Your honor, please note the timeline?" Larry pointed out. "People, the time on the screen is ten minutes before the shooting."

The camera spun around getting a view of the entire mall area.

"Hold up, hold up," he shouted. "Bailiff, please rewind that?" The bailiff did as he was instructed, replaying the last part of the video. "Look closely at that car right there. People, that's a beautiful Bentley Azure. Bailiff, can you zoom in? Look closely, the doors are opening up. Wait a minute, that looks like my client, if I'm not mistaken. Now look at the time, which is six minutes before the time of the shooting. Where's my client going?" he asked sarcastically. "He's walking into the restaurant behind that couple."

Justice was walking clear as day holding his cellphone to his ear. The camera showed him and the girl he came with standing at the desk, waiting to be seated. The girl was Dominique!

"Now, people, check the time now. It's two minutes before the shooting."

The crowd looked baffled as they watched Justice and Dom walking out of the restaurant an hour later, heading back to the car, then hopping in the car and pulling off.

"My client is just now leaving with his sister. What time does the screen say? That's an hour and two minutes after the shooting. Now show the other camera, please," he told the bailiff.

The bailiff hit the button, bringing up another image. The camera showed him pulling into a gas station and up to an air pump. He got out and pumped air into his tires.

"People, what time does the screen say?" Larry asked, pointing to the timeline. "That's now an hour and eight minutes after the crime. If I'm correct, the shooting has already taken place while he was in the restaurant eating. Now he is getting back into his car. Oh, wait a second, no he's not, he's standing there talking to someone on the phone."

The camera showed Justice talking on the phone. He paced back and forth before taking a seat on the trunk of his car. Justice was watching the video wondering how the hell he was in two places at one time, and with Dom, at that. That's when it all hit him. That was the reason his brother wouldn't come visit him at the prison or come to his court proceedings. It was also the reason why when Dom walked in, she gave him the thumbs up. He knew that was his brother letting him know everything was good. Justice watched on as his lawyer continued to put on a show.

"People, how can my client be in two places at the same time? What, was he cloned or has a double or something?"

"Only if you idiots knew!" Justice thought to himself.

Larry conceitedly placed his glasses on his face and walked back toward Justice. As he walked, he pointed his finger at Justice as if it was a gun. He then squeezed the imaginary trigger. "Bang," he whispered. "Killing 'em."

A huge grin appeared on Justice's face. He had to agree, Larry had just stuck a fork into the prosecutor's whole case. He looked back at Gabby, Dom, Chris, and Kreasha, who were all smiling ear to ear, and nodded his head.

"Hook, line, and sinker," he mumbled under his breath.

~ ~ ~

"Mr. Smith, please rise," the judge said, removing his glasses. "In light of this new evidence, and despite hearing testimony from the many different witnesses, it hurts me to say I have no choice but to dismiss the case against you. Mr. Smith, you are free to go."

The judge banged his gavel on the oak desk and left

the courtroom, saddened by the sudden chain of events. The prosecutor was even more pissed. Once again the great Larry Savino had done it. The federal agents sitting in the back stood up ice grilling Justice as they exited the courtroom. Justice smirked at them, feeling like he was untouchable.

"Thank you so much," Justice said, shaking Larry's hand.

"Just doing my job. I can tell by the look on your face you were doubting me. It was all part of the plan from the beginning. Your brother sacrificed a lot by helping out with this," Larry told him.

Supreme wanted to be at every hearing for his brother but couldn't risk it. He was the key piece to making the whole thing work. He cut his dreads off so they were identical again. That was him that was seen at the Cheesecake Factory and the gas station. He paid the managers ten thousand dollars apiece to recreate the timeline of the day of the shootings. He couldn't take a chance of the case going to trial. Altogether, the forty grand he had spent was well worth it.

“Mr. Smith, please come with us to fill out your paperwork,” the bailiff said.

“We’ll be outside when you finish,” Gabby replied, giving her man a deep and passionate kiss. “I have a surprise when you’re done,” she whispered in his ear.

“I can’t wait!” he told her, following the two bailiffs to the back.

EPILOGUE

Justice drove down the street in his new Cadillac truck. After getting out of a bad situation, he wanted to play it cool for awhile. The streets were praising him and his brother for the magic trick they performed. They really had the keys to the city now. Their plug handed over literally over sixty keys of heroin for free thanks to Chris saving his sister.

Justice wanted his brother to fall back from the operation and hopefully get the degree they had talked about, but Supreme loved what they had going right now. Justice believed this was the chance for Supreme to enroll into law school. He knew he would object to it, so he took the liberty to contact Supreme's old therapist, Karen, and together they were able to pull a few strings to make it happen. Now Justice had to deliver the good news.

"Yo, bro, where are you right now?" Justice asked

once Supreme answered.

"I'm just now getting off of I-95. What's up?"

"I need to talk to you," Justice said.

"I'll be there soon as I drop this money off to Chris. He was supposed to pick that shit up, but he's caught up with some bitch. We need to have a talk with him when we see him. MOB, bro, you know how we do," Supreme replied.

"Say no more! Anyway, make sure you stop past. I have some important news for you."

"No doubt," Supreme told him, ending the call.

Twenty minutes later, Supreme was driving down 5th and Cambria to meet up with Chris. Just as he was cruising through the stop sign, he heard sirens coming from behind him. When he looked in his rearview mirror, he saw the flashing lights.

"Fuck!" he said, pulling over.

Supreme eased his .40 cal. from his waist and slid it inside the glove compartment. He quickly locked it before the officer exited the car. He rolled the window down, hoping to get rid of the loud smell. He then reached in the side panel for his paperwork.

"What did I do, officer? I wasn't speeding or anything, so why am I being pulled over?" Supreme asked, staring up at the plain-clothes officers.

"You want to know what you did, huh?" the officer with the tie replied. "You and your bitch-ass lawyer tried to manipulate the system, but you're not above the law. Step out of the car, now!"

Supreme stepped out of the car and was pushed up against the hood. They searched him for anything illegal, but he was clean. They never searched his car, which told him they were just trying to harass him.

"Listen, I don't know what you're talking about," Supreme said. He knew they thought he was Justice, so he played along so they wouldn't find out.

"We will be keeping our eyes on you. You will slip up, and when you do, we'll be there to watch you fall for good. Enjoy the rest of your day," the other officer stated, letting him go.

They hopped in their unmarked car, then sped off. Supreme waited until they turned the corner before getting back into his car. He sat there emptying the contents of the Dutch out, then filled it with loud. Just as he was about to spark it, someone tapped on the window. Supreme looked up to see a gun aimed directly at his head. He never had the chance to do anything as the gunman fired a barrage of bullets into the car, hitting him with all seventeen shots.

The gunman then jumped in the approaching car and fled the scene. Supreme tried to move but couldn't. Through his heavy breathing, all he could think about was his brother and the little bit of time they had shared together. He wished he would have had the chance to talk to him one more time, but he didn't. That was the last thing he remembered before taking his last breath and falling into eternal darkness.

~ ~ ~

"It's done! Now you have to keep your end of the deal," the caller said.

"Don't tell me what I have to do, got it?"

"I was just saying," the caller began, but was cut off.

"You wasn't saying anything, you were just listening. I want my streets back by any means, and you're gonna help me get them. Are we clear?"

"Crystal!" the caller responded.

COMING SOON

MONEY MAKES ME CUM & .38 SPECIAL

Text Good2Go at 31996 to receive new release updates via text message

BOOKS BY GOOD2GO AUTHORS

SLUMPED
PART 1
JASON BRENT
GOOD 2 GO PUBLISHING PRESENTS
SILK WHITE
STRANDED
TEARS OF A HUSTLER
TEARS OF A HUSTLER 2
SILK WHITE
TEARS OF A HUSTLER 3
A NOVEL BY
SILK WHITE
TEARS OF A HUSTLER 4
YOU'VE BEEN WARNED
A NOVEL BY
SILK WHITE
SILKWHITE
TEARS OF A HUSTLER 5
THE SPADES
GOOD 2 GO PUBLISHING PRESENTS
SILKWHITE
TEARS OF A HUSTLER 6
THE TEFLON QUEEN
SILK WHITE
THE TEFLON QUEEN 2
SILK WHITE
THE TEFLON QUEEN 3
HARD TO KILL
SILK WHITE
THE TEFLON QUEEN 4
MR. DEATH
SILK WHITE
GOOD 2 GO PUBLISHING PRESENTS
THE TEFLON QUEEN 5
DEEP COVER
SILK WHITE
GOOD 2 GO PUBLISHING PRESENTS
THE TEFLON QUEEN
NO MERCY
SILK WHITE
THE PANTY RIPPER
REALITY WAY
GOOD 2 GO PUBLISHING PRESENTS
THE PANTY RIPPER
REALITY WAY
TIED TO A BOSS
J.L. ROSE
GOOD 2 GO PUBLISHING PRESENTS
TIME IS Money
Young Goonz
REALITY WAY

THE HACKMAN
NOW AVAILABLE ON YOUTUBE!

FILMS

To order books, please fill out the order form below:

To order films please go to www.good2gofilms.com

Name:____

Address:____

City: ____________ State: _____ Zip Code: ________________________

Phone:____

Email:____

Method of Payment: Check VISA MASTERCARD

Credit Card#:____

Name as it appears on card: __________________________________

Signature: ____

Item Name	Price	Qty	Amount
48 Hours to Die – Silk White	$14.99		
A Hustler's Dream - Ernest Morris	$14.99		
A Hustler's Dream 2 - Ernest Morris	$14.99		
Bloody Mayhem Down South	$14.99		
Business Is Business – Silk White	$14.99		
Business Is Business 2 – Silk White	$14.99		
Business Is Business 3 – Silk White	$14.99		
Childhood Sweethearts – Jacob Spears	$14.99		
Childhood Sweethearts 2 – Jacob Spears	$14.99		
Childhood Sweethearts 3 - Jacob Spears	$14.99		
Childhood Sweethearts 4 - Jacob Spears	$14.99		
Connected To The Plug – Dwan Marquis Williams	$14.99		
Flipping Numbers – Ernest Morris	$14.99		
Flipping Numbers 2 – Ernest Morris	$14.99		
He Loves Me, He Loves You Not - Mychea	$14.99		
He Loves Me, He Loves You Not 2 - Mychea	$14.99		
He Loves Me, He Loves You Not 3 - Mychea	$14.99		
He Loves Me, He Loves You Not 4 – Mychea	$14.99		
He Loves Me, He Loves You Not 5 – Mychea	$14.99		
Lord of My Land – Jay Morrison	$14.99		
Lost and Turned Out – Ernest Morris	$14.99		
Married To Da Streets – Silk White	$14.99		
M.E.R.C. - Make Every Rep Count Health and Fitness	$14.99		
My Besties – Asia Hill	$14.99		
My Besties 2 – Asia Hill	$14.99		
My Besties 3 – Asia Hill	$14.99		
My Besties 4 – Asia Hill	$14.99		
My Boyfriend's Wife - Mychea	$14.99		
My Boyfriend's Wife 2 – Mychea	$14.99		
My Brothers Envy – J. L. Rose	$14.99		
Naughty Housewives – Ernest Morris	$14.99		
Naughty Housewives 2 – Ernest Morris	$14.99		
Naughty Housewives 3 – Ernest Morris	$14.99		
Naughty Housewives 4 – Ernest Morris	$14.99		

ERNEST MORRIS

Never Be The Same – Silk White	$14.99		
Stranded – Silk White	$14.99		
Slumped – Jason Brent	$14.99		
Supreme & Justice – Ernest Morris	$14.99		
Supreme & Justice 2 – Ernest Morris	$14.99		
Tears of a Hustler - Silk White	$14.99		
Tears of a Hustler 2 - Silk White	$14.99		
Tears of a Hustler 3 - Silk White	$14.99		
Tears of a Hustler 4- Silk White	$14.99		
Tears of a Hustler 5 – Silk White	$14.99		
Tears of a Hustler 6 – Silk White	$14.99		
The Panty Ripper - Reality Way	$14.99		
The Panty Ripper 3 – Reality Way	$14.99		
The Solution – Jay Morrison	$14.99		
The Teflon Queen – Silk White	$14.99		
The Teflon Queen 2 – Silk White	$14.99		
The Teflon Queen 3 – Silk White	$14.99		
The Teflon Queen 4 – Silk White	$14.99		
The Teflon Queen 5 – Silk White	$14.99		
The Teflon Queen 6 - Silk White	$14.99		
The Vacation – Silk White	$14.99		
Tied To A Boss - J.L. Rose	$14.99		
Tied To A Boss 2 - J.L. Rose	$14.99		
Tied To A Boss 3 - J.L. Rose	$14.99		
Tied To A Boss 4 - J.L. Rose	$14.99		
Tied To A Boss 5 - J.L. Rose	$14.99		
Time Is Money - Silk White	$14.99		
Two Mask One Heart – Jacob Spears and Trayvon Jackson	$14.99		
Two Mask One Heart 2 – Jacob Spears and Trayvon Jackson	$14.99		
Two Mask One Heart 3 – Jacob Spears and Trayvon Jackson	$14.99		
Wrong Place Wrong Time	$14.99		
Young Goonz – Reality Way	$14.99		
Subtotal:			
Tax:			
Shipping (Free) U.S. Media Mail:			
Total:			

Make Checks Payable To:
Good2Go Publishing
7311 W Glass Lane,
Laveen, AZ 85339

CPSIA information can be obtained
at www.ICGtesting.com
Printed in the USA
LVHW02s0840281017
554098LV00008BA/73/P